Jesus
and
Peter

Jesus
and
Peter

A Different Account Of Christ
And His Catholic Church

BY
Barry Leonardini

REGENT PRESS
Berkeley, California

[paperback]
ISBN-13: 978-1-58790-567-4
ISBN 10: 1-58790-567-1

[e-book]
ISBN-13: 978-1-58790-569-8
ISBN 10: 1-58790-569-8

Libray of Congress Control Number: 2021933642

MANUFACTURED IN THE UNITED STATES OF AMERICA

REGENT PRESS
Berkeley, California
www.regentpress.nbet

Contents

CHAPTER ONE

Jesus Is Brought To Pontius Pilate

The Roman governor's accommodations were a stark example of the rich culture of the Roman Empire. The sharp, thoughtful, symmetrical architecture was made more vivid by the lack of those qualities in the surrounding indigenous local buildings. Pontius Pilate lived in a ten acre compound surrounded by a twelve foot high, four foot thick wall. The concentric allocation of space ranged from the most private being in the center. Further away form that sanctum was increasingly more public space. The Roman guards would populate and secure the most outer regions. The hearing that Pilate would conduct with Jesus would be held in a public court room. It had a high ceiling and many windows. The windows could be shuttered for inclement weather. Pilate's seat was on a raised dais.

Behind him on the wall was displayed SPQR. That sign of authority gave Pilate's judgments the stamp of approval as per the Senate and People of Rome. Marble was not abundant, so the Roman corp of engineers made do with scented Cedars of Lebanon and Aleppo pine from Syria for wall and ceiling construction. The marble was saved for flooring.

Pilate was an aristocratic looking man. He had a Roman nose that if it had a little more down and under to its tip, would have been the envy of the Roman eagle mascot of the empire. He was in his late forties. Like all Roman aristocrats, he spent time as an officer in the Roman legions. The lines in his handsome face along with the deliberate gestures of his body movements suggested a self assured cosmopolitan man. He was trim yet muscular. He is impeccably dressed. In fact he is over dressed for the likes of most of the locals that come before him. Why was he in Jerusalem? Why wasn't he in Rome? Was it something he did or said that landed him in this dung heap of a country? Who could possibly be rewarded by being an arbiter of grievances between obnoxious, lying and stinking Jews? Pilate was surrounded by two scribes. One scribe was to recite evidence that was gathered against the accused. The other scribe would take notes of testimony. There were also six guards and a personal equerry. The aid offered Pilate a drink of water. Pilate accepted.

Then an imperious and world weary Pilate addresses Jesus, "The only thing more over rated than man is his over rated Gods. Now I am informed that you are both man and God. I am rhetorically speechless." Pilate theatrically pauses. Then like an eagle in a stoop towards a hapless rabbit he glares at Jesus with his cold blue eyes and says, "Please guide me through your marvelous hybrid being." Jesus doesn't respond. It's as if he is unfamiliar with a person with the stature of Pontius Pilate.

Pilate, looking slightly irritated, tries a different tact. He notices remnants of his own wardrobe. What's left of the Tyrian purple cape, the gold thread sandals and the exotic scents of his own personal favorite cologne show up on Christ. "Do we shop at the same stores?" Jesus now knows where his clothes came from. How embarrassing. Peter and John have made him more vulnerable because the judge now has correctly prejudged him. He is thrown off balance because Pilate has him accurately identified as a common thief who received stolen property from Pilate's own household.

Finally Jesus speaks, "I did not claim to be the Messiah or the son of God. That was an idea of my producers. Bring them here. They will tell you." "It will surprise you to know that Peter, one of your producers, has told my investigators that you, Jesus, wrote all your own material. He also said that you were told by both producers that you would be presented as the Messiah. Scribe, what's the other producers name?"

The scribe answers, "His name was John. We can't find him. We were told he ran away with the first act in Jesus' sermon. She was known as Nefrateri the torch singer. He may be in Egypt. There was some talk of him teaming up with Nefrateri's family in Egypt. They are in wheat and want to hedge their crops. John suggested a futures market based on different degrees of Nile flooding. The more flooding then the better chance of bumper crops and the less flooding . . . "

An irritated Pilate jumps in, "Yes. Yes. Never mind all that. And so Jesus, you were told by both John and Peter that you would be marketed as the Messiah. That's the 'promised one.' So you steal clothes and you steal identities. How do you plead? Guilty or not guilty?"

"Who brings these charges?" Jesus asks in a raised voice.

Pilate instructs the scribe, "Show Jesus the complaint. You will see that it is stamped with the seal of the Sanhedrin and underscored by the signatures of various members of that body. The signatories include Shyster or was it Warlock? No it's Shylock. Also Uriah Heep, Fagin and Theodor Herzl have signed. They are the rabbis that control the Sanhedrin. They are also influential among the other local Jews who are in business in Jerusalem. The complaint in its essence indicts you for blasphemy. That's punishable by death according to Jewish law. But they cannot execute you. Rome is the controlling government in Jerusalem so it's our responsibility to carry out capital crimes execution. As for the stolen clothes. I make no complaint. And I don't want them back. By the way, are you a Jew? You could pass for a patrician in clean clothes and clean shaven and if you kept your mouth shut."

"My mother is Jewish and I think that the man she says is my father is not my real father. I think my real father served in the Roman legion that was stationed here some thirty 36 years ago."

Pilate interrupts, "Do you have any proof of that claim of a Roman father?" Jesus shakes his head no.

Pilate says, "So never mind that. Without proof of a Roman connection you are liable to Jewish laws. Let's explore your philosophy. I had some scribes attend your recent sermon. They wrote down what you were advocating. It's news to me some of your views and conclusions. For example, you talk about 'the meek.' You said and I quote, *'Blessed are the meek for they shall possess the earth.'* I ask you Jesus, are you meek?"

Jesus answers, "I am meek."

Pilate pounces ever so softly, "Carrying on as the son of God in public whether you truly believed it or if it was only an expedient is not meek. Rather it's an arrogance of showmanship and a grasp for power. Why do the meek deserve to possess the earth?"

"The meek use only what is necessary for their daily survival. They do not spend time accumulating wealth. One person only eat one meal at a time. Why waste time and deprive others of food by gathering too much? Also I took no money for my performances," protested Christ.

"You got more than money. You got a total life support from your producers. You want for nothing. The fact that no money came to you is a feeble defense. It's only because you didn't ask for it. And that reminds me of another outlandish position that you preached the other night. And I quote, *'Ask, and it shall be given you, seek and you shall find, knock and it shall be* opened to you. For everyone who asks shall receive and he who seeks shall find and he that knocks the door will be opened.' There's more but I am curious. Have you ever held a job. Have you ever sweated in pursuit of a building project?"

"I helped out in my families work shop."

"What would your family do if someone came into your families place of business and simply asked for some goods without offering payment?" Jesus responds, "My family would refuse service and set a price."

"Suppose you were alone in the shop and a customer came in and asked for some goods. Would you give them goods without payment?"

"No. I don't have the authority."

Pilate asks, "Then why do you preach this foolhardy tactic of merely asking others for goods and services as a plausible way to live a life?"

"It's my philosophy."

"Where did you learn such a philosophy?"

"I studied in the east. I made myself familiar with the Buddhists religion."

Pilate looks at Jesus with a surprised look of pleasure, "Eureka! Now I see a connection and logic to your behavior. You are spoiled like the Gautama Buddha was. Do you know the background of the of the

13

founder of Buddhist philosophy?"

Jesus answers, "No."

"I learned about him from a friend of mine in the Roman foreign office. He was stationed in Persia or Assyria some years ago. He, the Buddha, was spoiled like you are. His father was a king in India. He was kept away from the general society and schooled in private. It was the fathers hope that the boy would become a great king and thus should be shielded from religion and petty politics. That may have been unwise, but that's not important right now. I can tell that you have been spoiled. Your father and mother weren't royals. But poor people can spoil children also. Anyway, Buddha leaves home and sees first hand his fathers kingdom. It smells. The people suffer. So Buddha leaves the palace and renounces his riches and birthright. He goes about the realm preaching self esteem and an assertiveness in getting from nature what is enough and not letting royal families tell you that you do not deserve equality. Buddha was advocating a middle way between conspicuous consumption and chosen poverty. Let's see if I can remember? Oh yes. My friend used as an example the Buddha contemplating the tuning of a lute to relate the message of the proper middle way of living. A lute string too tight is as a bad as a string too loose. Both miss the pitch of harmony. It's actually another way of saying what the Greeks have said all long — nothing to excess. Leave it to the Greeks to be in the top list of originators. Now getting back to personal ideas and experiences. When you were in India, did Buddhists give you things by merely asking them?"

"Sometimes."

"How can you preach a life's philosophy that sometimes doesn't work?"

Jesus responds, "Now who's the naïve one? Isn't philosophy by definition an art in lowering expectations? Doesn't that match life's experience? Any philosophy that preaches perfection doesn't work almost all of the time. One can work, but sometimes work does not get one where one wants to go. One can rest, but that's a fruitless experience. But if one chooses a balance of work and leisure then both are enhanced and compliment each other."

An arrogant Pilate storms back, "So that's the way you see things? You are a pompous dilettante. You tell your followers merely to be meek as if it's the goal to achieve. You don't tell them to work hard. You don't tell them to save for a rainy day. You and your followers remind me of the country Hibernia. The Celts live on that island. Have you ever heard of the Celts?

Jesus shakes his no. He's never heard of the Celts.

Pilate continues, "I commanded a legion during the reign of Augustus. I was stationed in Britannia. Caledonia was in the north of Britannia. But off the west coast of Britannia was a country called Hibernia inhabited by the Celts. I was ordered to do a reconnaissance in strength. My commanders wanted to know about the peoples and the assets on the island. I found the people much like I find the Jews. They were argumentative and quick to blame others for their shortcomings. They even blamed the bad weather on their neighbors. I can't remember the stupid argument. But they also wanted something for nothing. They also didn't have any architecture worth mentioning. Their food was also poor. They had one thing in abundance and that was politics. They debated politics all day long while drinking a fermented brew. I swear that one day a Celt was pro a certain argument and on the very next day he was con that same argument because some one else had showed up at the public house. So here I am stuck where the dust of Jerusalem replaces the rain of Kildaire. But the two cultures are balanced with equal amounts of banality. I reported back to my commanders that the island possessed some physical assets but the native population was more trouble than it was worth. And you couldn't get a straight answer to any question without a verbal fight of Homeric proportions. I recommended no invasion." Pilate continues, "How did you spend time in growing up?"

"As I said, I traveled to the east. I learned about other religions."

"Did you travel alone? How old were you?"

"I left home when I was thirteen. Prior to that, my mother had provided me a Greek tutor who was from Ephesus. He included eastern studies with my basic instructions. His first hand experiences in the east sparked an appetite for my wander lust. His tales of the grand civilizations of India and Persia made me anxious to witness them first hand. From then on I was bored with the Jerusalem. So I hitched a ride with a caravan that was going east. I left a note of farewell to my mother. I told her I would return. I traveled in India and other places for 18 years."

Pilate asks, "Weren't you concerned for your mother's feelings because of your abrupt departure?"

"Deep inside of me, I felt my leaving was for the best. She knew that I was suspicious of Joseph being my real father. A quick relief for the shared embarrassment would be for me to just leave the scene. She would be hurt. But she would also be relieved."

"And what did life in the east teach you?"

"The first impression was the magnificent civilization and culture. The architecture rivaled Romes. The food was complex and tasty. The women were beautiful. There were under classes of society that were immediately apparent. I became house help for a group of Buddhist monks. I had my own room and was fed twice a day in return for my simple labors. I didn't speak their language, but my chores were simple enough to not require conversation. A motion to do this or that was sufficient to get me in the routine. The monks also taught me of their religion. They were low keyed. It was the religion of Buddha. Buddhism is simple. It advises that we must trust in God. He will provide. But the monks taught it differently. They did not say trust in God specifically. They were taught and they practiced mutual caring. They quietly asked for food, clothing, shelter and medicines. People would respond and that would store value of good will or karma with the monks. The monks in turn would do good works for other people who were in need. The message is to be good you must do good. That was their goal. I added that it was also God's message. My message was tailored to have continuity with the upbringing of God fearing Jews. I guess that's what upset the rabbis and that's why I am here today. "

Pilate asks, "Explain karma."

"It refers to the consequences of ones life. I said before I heard of the word karma 'One reaps what one sows.' But the Indians were way ahead of me. They reduced the description of the concept to one word thousands of years ago." "'Trust in God.' That's something I was curious about when I saw the reports of your sermon. Let's see here." Pilate examines the sheets. "Here it is. And I quote. *Therefore do not be anxious, saying, What shall we eat? Or what shall we drink? Or what shall we put on? For the father knows you need these things. But seek first the kingdom of God and his justice and all these things shall be given to you besides.'* In other words, 'Trust in God.' Did you say those words?"

Jesus nods, "Yes. I said those words."

Pilate continues, "So what you really meant was to trust in God but also beg for help as per the Indian Buddhists? But you didn't mention Buddhism. It might have turned out entirely different for you if you honestly said that you represented an Indian religion. There's no harm in that. But to shade the peoples religion with this new twist of trust in God alienated vested powers. It also confused the common folk. In short you have caused a mess by this omission of the origin of your beliefs. The Sanhedrin have a valid complaint."

Jesus answers proudly, "Yes, I added trust in God for he will provide to the fundamental Buddhist philosophy of being good by doing good. That seems to be minutiae compared to the good my words seemed to have accomplished." Pilate added, "But the ends do not justify the means. Did you teach or pick up a following in India like you have here in Jerusalem?"

"No. I would be redundant there. The monks had those people trained already. I was merely support for the monks. I brought those experiences back to Jerusalem. I wanted to start my own branch of their life style."

Pilate speaks, "Begging for help is a kind of mock work. But it's not the same as sweat and planning. Self esteem goes away. Sloth and bitterness creep in and take the place of self reliance. It would appear that you came by your ignorance of the value of work honestly. Neither your mother nor your father ever explained it to you. Nor did they require you to perform any. But ignorance is no excuse for misinforming people of the value of honest effort that produces tangible results. That's different from begging which redistributes other's work-earned wealth. Look at the ceiling in this room." Pilate motions at the architecture." I have news. God did not provide this ceiling. Roman engineers and carpenters built this ceiling. They built this compound and they built the Roman Empire. Do you think yourself a realist?"

"Why do you feel threatened by me? Why am I here? You are being used Pilate. The people who want me removed are the local rabbis who are in the business of faith and worship. They make money selling animals for slaughter. They make a profit soliciting alms for the poor by holding back a hefty percentage of what's given. I trashed their banking quarters and they want me dead. They call it a temple but it is a palace of lies. It also changes money for a profit. Real people who have a real faith in an almighty do not need a place to go to pray. But there's no money in that. So the so called religious leaders provide a building to pray and sacrifice for those who had rather be seen doing acts of worship rather than actually doing acts of worship in private. Superficial people wont do things unless they have a witness. They are always trying to profit some how from their efforts."

Pilate is engaged by what Jesus says are the real motives of the Sanhedrin. He asks, "Then you renounce the claim of being the son of God?"

"Yes I do. It was never my idea in the first place. My producers, Peter and John, wanted me to take on the persona of Messiah. I made a bad bargain. I thought I could use them to get my honest and simple message out to the people. But ironically they used me more than I used them. Peter and John and others are as greedy as the Sanhedrin. They are using me to start a new religion that's based on mandated equality for all."

Pilate responds, "Mandated equality for everyone? Oh. So they want to model your new religion on the Greek democracy model. Blending secular government with religion, isn't that clever? Now if the government/church decide to raise taxes it becomes a religious act. They are only doing Gods work by redistributing other's fruits of labor to those who may not choose to work. What's next? Maybe they don't stop at just wealth redistribution. They could now pass laws that make any of the under class of people more entitled because of the mere fact that they need or are disabled. Or they are a certain sex or a certain religion or maybe they are handicapped. One is poor, therefore one has been abused, therefore one who is richer has to pay a penalty. One is handicapped so everyone must walk slower or think slower so the handicapped can keep up. Maybe the handicapped can now compete in games but no score will be kept so as not to show disrespect or elitism or embarrass the handicapped. Heaven help us if we tell them what we think of them. Meritocracy is replaced with a celebration of the mentally and physically deficient. The possibility for chaos is infinite. Now that is truly dangerous. I am sure that the Roman Senate wouldn't like that development.

That's why Rome was set up as a Republic and not a democracy. Tiberius would even be more upset. It seems Jesus that you are in over your head. You are between greedy downtown established rabbis and your very ambitious producer wannabees. You are in mortal danger. And both of your enemies want me to the dirty work. The rabbis don't want the competition. And I am sorry to inform you that my sources feel Peter thinks you would be more valuable to him as a dead martyr to kick start his new religious and secular business. Martyrdom is a big selling point to morons who can't critically assess people and their motives and understand their beliefs. The simplistic slobs think since Jesus is dead he must have been right and worthy of our adoration. Aren't people disappointing?" "What's to become of me? What's the penalty for blasphemy. Can't you see that I have been taken in by the producers? Please show mercy. Talk to Shylock, Heep and Fagin and the others. Tell them I will stop meeting with people and I will go away."

Pilate is somewhat touched, "I will try to reason with them. You have done nothing wrong that merits a forfeit of your life. But blasphemy is punishable by crucifixion. And crucifixion can be in two ways. Either by nails through the hands and feet which causes bleeding to death and excruciating pain and dehydration. Or the other method is to merely tie the person to the cross until one dies of exposure. I can rule on the method. I would advise the latter one. Then I could have one of the guards pierce you in the heart shortly after you have been crucified. The lance will bring quick closure to the whole affair. It's your choice."

"Aren't you going to try to get the charges dropped?" pleads Jesus.

"Have you met Shylock? Have you heard about Shylock?"

"No," Jesus replies.

Pilate asks in a snarl, "Have you ever tried to reason or bargain with an insect? These people are a desert breed of insect. Their natural greed and keenness enhances their survival in the desert. But when they are among more affluent civilizations and the surrounding abundance they try to grasp more than they need and they go from insects to pigs."

Jesus' face drops, "So it's that way, is it?"

"I am afraid so. Shylock, Heep and Fagin are in the next room. Would you want to be present when I plead your case or would like to wait in another room?"

"I prefer to be present."

Pilate motions to a guard, "Bring in the members of the Sanhedrin."

The guard escorts the three middle aged men into the room. Shylock leads the other two. He's the tallest but he still doesn't come up to the chin of Jesus. In descending order Heep is smaller, followed by Fagin who is the smallest. Pilate notices immediately that the difference in height between the first and the second rabbi and the second and the third rabbi is proportionally the same. Pilate also marks that their physical characteristics and the quality and abundance of their robes and their jewelry also gradually and proportionally descend as per their rank. They all have an equal, dark and weathered complexion. Pilate speculates that the wrinkles and furls on their face could reflect a life of calculating what is owed or what can be got by a different no cash down way. Shylock has the most gold chains. The chains are all different styles. It suggests that he may be a part time pawnbroker and that his personal adornments are the result of many pawn tickets not redeemed. His face is spare. Only enough skin to form a face is used. Except for the nose which grandly precedes and isn't proportional to what follows. When one is a desert breed a sharp nose can make the difference between water and food or starvation.

Heep and Fagin are variations on Shylock's theme. When they walk the chains clink and chime quasi musically. Pilate muses to himself. Could he choreograph a musical entertainment using the three and the bell tones they produce? He knows a perfect name already. He would call them, "The Bells That Will Take a Toll." Wistfully Pilate thinks about what his life in Rome's legions and the following public service has amounted to. He doesn't have to think long. It hasn't been what he had hoped. He's admitted to himself for some time now that a life following the Muses would have been more fulfilling. He's an accomplished harp and lute player. He's a graceful dancer. He's written stage plays in his spare time and also did some acting and directing in the academy of Rome while growing up. Maybe it's not too late. It's now or never. As soon as possible he will plan a trip to Rome and plan an try to arrange an early retirement as soon as he can be replaced.

But now he has a nasty chore. He's sorry for Jesus. He will do what he can to get the charges dismissed by the Sanhedrin, or make the best deal for Jesus that's possible so as to mitigate any further pain for the well meaning naive free spirit. Shylock and the two rabbis face Pilate. They are on the left and Jesus is on the right.

"Welcome honorable members of the Sanhedrin. This is Jesus. I have spoken with Jesus at length. It's clear to me that this young man has committed no crime. In fact, it would appear that he himself has been a victim of unscrupulous theatrical producers. I think it would be in every ones interests to drop the complaint. What do you say?"

Shylock acknowledges Jesus with a simple glance. Heep and Fagin are motionless but with a sense of resolution. They know what they want and they won't leave until they get it.

"Why would we drop the complaint? Did he or did he not support the idea that he was the Messiah?"

Pilate answers, "Jesus has denied ever claiming that title. He says that Peter and John are the producers who pushed that public persona to the people as a way to attract larger audiences. It was all about promotion."

"We of the Sanhedrin have settled with Peter. John is nowhere to be found."

Pilate is piqued. The fact that these insects are picking and choosing which of the equally guilty in the Messiah affair will be prosecuted lowers Pilate to the status of a garbage man who responds to hasty calls of service — "Hey you, take this out and let this stay." The Sanhedrin has challenged his authority and self esteem. That won't be tolerated. He'd rather cleave their sculls then follow their dictates. That seals it. He is fed up with his position in the greater Roman government. He wants out. It's a life with the muses as soon as possible. Imperious Pilate glares at Shylock with revulsion. If looks could kill, Shylock would be in flames.

"What kind of deal did you make with Peter?"

"Peter has reimbursed us for the mess that Jesus made in the temple. I don't know whether you heard of it? But this man released the sacrificial animals. Birds and goats ran out. Some goats were caught, but the pigeons all got away. He also over turned our money-changing tables. Some money is still missing and the tables were scratched. Peter also gave us his signed deposition that Jesus was the mastermind behind the son of God plot. We have no complaint against Peter. We reserve the right to bring charges against John."

"Your legal conclusions fail logic. Your greed for compensation of damages and desire for revenge on

Jesus doesn't justify the zig zag application of the laws. If you drop charges against Peter because he pays you money, why can't Jesus also pay and go free? Peter was part of the whole scheme. Your charge of Jesus' blasphemy claiming to be the Messiah is a capital offense. Peter was part of that scheme no matter what defense he claims. Therefore Peter will also be crucified. His deposition is worthless. Now how say you? Will you also send Peter to the cross so you can get to Jesus?"

"Take Peter. He's yours. But I think he has fled to Rome with this social contagion religious-philosophy. Rome deserves this flu. It will cause its demise in the years ahead," says Shylock immediately.

Jesus thinks that Peter finally got what he wanted. He got out of Jerusalem. Pilate is somewhat stunned by Shylock's intensity of greed and purpose. He speculates that there is something more to this Messiah affair that the Sanhedrin are frightened of.

"Fess up. Tell me truthfully of your fears that motivate this blood lust for Jesus. What does he say that frightens you so?" Shylock responds, "He threatens our power and he threatens our religion. Ultimately he threatens the Roman Empire. And that includes you and your own position noble Pilate."

"Which is more important to you at the Sanhedrin?"

Pilate cynically asks.

"First my honorable governor, let me refer to the articles of Romes occupation, to which we of the Sanhedrin are a personal signatory. The articles do not provide the representative of Rome the right to question the motives of the legitimate government of the occupied. So long as Rome's interests are not interfered with we can carry on around here for what passes as the new normal. We pay you and Rome taxes for this unwelcome occupation. Therefore we respectfully say to you that our judgment on Jesus is legally none of your business. But in deference to you and the power that belongs to Rome, whether that is logical or not, we will give you Peter as a gesture of fair play. Do with him what you choose. But to answer your more important question of what really motivates our fear of Jesus I will answer truthfully. Your cultured and imperious Roman ear doesn't hear the sedition and revolution that is just beneath the surface of the words of Jesus. Your imperial culture has developed a compensating blind spot to the occupied lands and their people. In short you have so much that the little things escape you.

I know and feel your deep revulsion for me and my associates. I know you think me an insect of the desert. Your body movements speak honestly of what you privately think. Your tone of voice and the demeanor you take towards me scream your distaste. But I say to you indeed I am a desert insect. I make no excuses. I was one before you and Rome showed up. And I will be one after you and Rome leave. If you didn't like or now don't like desert insects why did you come or why do you still stay? This is a place of desert insects. If you don't like it either leave or kill us all. Or is the real motivation something else? Does it really point to more of a desire to tax desert insects and put up with the ambient desert insect culture and demote lofty imperial culture into a position that will tolerate talking and dealing with insects so you can have the fruit of insect labor? Your words say one thing but your actions speak louder. So what does that say about you Romans, Emperor Tiberius, the Roman Senate and your imperial self image? It implies that you all are willing to have bugs in the kitchen. And if some bugs fall into the soup it's just a cost of the empire business. The bugs can live in the kitchen where your food is prepared. You may sometimes eat an occasional bug without knowing it. But never mind it. As long as there are no bugs on the gold leaf plates or golden utensils when it arrives at the table. At least the ones someone can spot. Lest I get to far afield with my insect venom I will come to the point. Simply the fact is that Jesus claims to be the Messiah and the son of God and his message preaches leisure without work. Western cultures celebrated Greek philosopher Aristotle said, "One must work to have leisure." But Jesus wants no part of it. He's a spoiled brat who preaches a trust in God or trust in nature to supply what's really important. There is no discipline or work ethic in his words. What do you think the morons who listen to him will take away from his speech. They will figure that someone will provide. Whether that be God, nature or some one with power and wealth. And that will be the beginning of the end for civilization as we all now know it. That will effect us and the contagion will eventually engulf the Roman Empire.

This is not a local issue. If you and I don't stamp it out, it will not only bring down the Sanhedrin it will also work its way throughout the whole Roman Empire. What do you think Emperor Tiberius and the Roman Senate would think about a provincial governor who is trying to give a pass to deadbeat Messiah and his deadbeat followers whose philosophy basically preaches less or no work as an inalienable right, a right assumed at birth. So with each tick higher in the population the count of a new batch of entitled will grow. They will be screaming outside the doors of government and the wealthy — "We want more." Tiberius and the Senate wouldn't take longer than a Roman minute to off you and Jesus and any one else that's near by. You are expendable my dear governor. Jesus would die immediately. But you would wish you were dead because of the back water that you would be reassigned to. In case I haven't made myself clear, here it is in a nutshell. The taxed desert insects would become consumers of tax revenues because of the welfare that the followers of Jesus' church would demand. I ask you. How are you going to maintain a sprawling empire on that business model?"

Pilate is uncharacteristically speechless. What an eloquent presentation Shylock articulated. And he's right about the logical extension of the teachings of Jesus. People would just boot responsibility. Forget heroes. Forget merit. Forget following the rules. That would all fall under elitist goals. And if one was a member of the elite then one could be classified as a abuser of the poor or handicapped. That's how worthless people could game a democracy coupled with religion. That could happen. But what about simple Jesus? His naive feel-good philosophy has merit. But the people he talks to hear only what they want to hear.

It's possible that as many that would honestly work would be off balanced by an equal number who would work less or not work at all because they felt it was their God- given right to game the system of welfare and social safety nets.

Pilate asks, "But how will Tiberius and the Roman Senate hear of Jesus? "

Shylock answers, "We have polled and accumulated depositions of sermon attendees and what their take away was of the teachings of Jesus. At least seventy-five percent state that they will have to work less and worry less under a future with a Jesus philosophy directing the government. We have advertising posters of Jesus' sermons that have catch phrases such as 'Fire your boss, there is less work in your future.' We have copies of his speeches that indict Jesus in his own words. We merely copied down his *What me Worry?* proverbs. Included are his praising of the meek. He also instructs that the sick and handicapped must first be taken care of before any one else can advance or enjoy life. He may make a good lecturer on a cruise ship but as a leader of a new religion that's coupled to the secular government he's a fermenting bomb. We have copies of these depositions in the hands of couriers right now. They are some distance away from us at this moment. They await my recall command. We also have told the couriers that if they don't get word from us by tomorrow noon that they are to deliver the documents to Rome. To Rome with love. The Caesars boast that 'All roads lead to Rome" is valid. But by definition the roads are a two-way street. I'm sorry I resorted to this tactic. But that's how desert insects behave."

"Who would care about what goes on in Jerusalem? Who would care about the trial of a hippy Jew named Jesus? And if such a person did exist in Rome, how would you find him? And how would that person make use of this information?" asked Pilate in a somewhat more respectful voice.

"My first thought is a cousin of mine who passes for white and is employed in the Provinces Affairs judicial department. He was the issue of a similar out of wedlock love affair between a local Jewess and a Roman officer assigned to an Egyptian building inventory attachment. I know he would personally love your job. But if he couldn't come back here for a while, he would shop this dossier through the halls of the entire Forum complex until he found someone. Pilate, there are plenty people in Rome that would take your place either willingly or be forced to. A couple examples would include a minister in the sewers projects of

Rome. He would gladly trade that territory for clean desert air. Another example would be to go to the higher offices inhabited by the more powerful patricians in Roman society. I'll bet many of them would love to get rid of greedy sons-in-laws or annoying siblings by having them shipped to Jerusalem. They wouldn't study the merits of the case of Jesus. They would just see the opportunity to dump their particular problem by dumping you. And then replacing you with some one who would do what the laws of occupation required. In the end Jesus would still be dead anyway. But this way, with you merely following what the law requires all the possible messy fall out to your reputation and job are avoided. So it has to be. Jesus goes and you stay. Unless you want to go with Jesus?"

"I want to be alone with Jesus. Please leave. I will notify you shortly. Thank you for your input."

The members of the Sanhedrin leave the room as they had entered. Only now in reverse with the same amount of lock steps and the same height proportionally spacing in a line.

Pilate turns to Jesus, "They've legally got me over a barrel. Jesus this looks bad for you. But I swear that Peter will be crucified. And it will be a long excruciating ordeal. If I can catch him. He is on his way to

Rome. He's taken your message to the capitol in the hopes of starting your church. The only thing I can do for you is to arrange a lax security in your cell block. You must contact your friends. You can have unlimited visitors at any time. You must arrange an escape."

"I only preached loving ways of living. What's wrong with that?" asks a sorrowful Jesus.

"Basically, your claim to be the son of God or the Messiah makes the Sanhedrin redundant. If you are who the producers claim you are then Shylock and company have lost their franchise. From being the boss they face the prospect of being without a job. Frankly I'm fed up with my position as governor any way. So Shylock's threat to have me recalled doesn't really bother me. But he is indeed accurate that my replacement will certainly put you to death. So it's already out of my hands. That's why I advise you to escape. If you force me into an execution I can only promise a quick death after you are on the cross. As I've offered, I will have one of the guards lance you in the heart. It will then be over in an instant. But please try to escape."

Jesus face tells it all. He is broken and despondent. "I never claimed absolutely that I was the son of God. I will admit not stopping talk that claimed my divinity.

But for everyone who thought me the Messiah there were more who thought me a fake. I did not think it a good way to start my talks with disclaimers. My message was important whether the Son of God was talking or a hippy Jew was speaking."

Pilate says, "You were doomed from the beginning. Your message indicted you more than your producers controversial claim that you were the Messiah. Your preachings of trust in God and laying up riches in heaven and relying on others to support people in need scares the hell out of the powers that run Jerusalem. And it will make the Emperor and the Roman Senate even more upset. You made two errors. Either one by themselves sealed your fate. You can't preach to people that they don't have to work. And you shouldn't claim to be the son of God. Do you advocate a democracy? Are you a democrat?"

Jesus interrupts, "I did not say one didn't have to work. And no I am not a democrat. I have absolutely no political ambitions."

"Maybe not exactly. But you forgot you were speaking to adults who have on average the education of an eight year old. It sounded like you gave them a pass to put work into a secondary category behind enjoying the good life first, whatever the 'good life' meant to the different people who were listening. I'll wager each had their own interpretation. You are guilty of being naïve. That is for sure. It's sad that fault now demands the death penalty. People who live by others efforts cannot survive without taxes or some kind of slavery. Your teachings threaten them. You are also a rugged individualist. Governments don't want too many rugged individualists because they make the natives restless with their sporty behavior. Maybe you can tell me how you came by these foreign ideas?" Jesus answers, "It started a relatively short time ago on the shores of the Sea of Galilee . . . "

CHAPTER II
Back To The Beginning . . .
Peter Meets Apostles
Peter and John

erusalem is located in the middle of ancient trade routes and theaters of war between peoples that have a rich cultural heritage. Included are Egyptians, Phoenicians, Syrians (Syria is oldest continuous inhabited area on earth), Sumerians, Babylonians, Armenians, Carthaginians and recently the occupying Romans. Geographically speaking, one can't miss going into Jerusalem while traveling in that general locale. Aesthetically speaking one can easily miss going to Jerusalem and not suffer any loss. It is surrounded by land that many visit but don't stay long and definitely would not choose to live.

The terrain is poor in quality. The land shapes the culture of the people who inhabit it. Consequently, the indigenous Palestinians and Jews don't have much culture. There is no architecture. There is no science that wasn't imported. The music can't be whistled or hummed. Clothing only covers the body. The jewelry belonged to some one else or some other culture first. The philosophers stopped lowering expectations because of no room. The government isn't paid any mind because there isn't anything to vote for because there isn't anything left to redistribute. Literature is found only in the foreign books section of the library in nearby Egypt. The surrounding area of Jerusalem is largely unsuitable for growing crops on a large scale. Consequently the local diet is more about eating fish, sheep or goat with some additional fiber. The Palestinians and Jews bus tables, operate bazaars, catch fish and slaughter animals for the menus of their inns. They compensate for their poor heritage by telling grossly exaggerated lies about their ancestors and their respective Gods. Why would any God claim these two peoples? And if some God did claim them, why would he let them live in this arm pit of a country? To hear the Jews tell the story, they were here before there was a before. The Palestinians say that there was a before and it was named Philistia and the Palestinians were originally Philistines. Only because newcomers slurred or mispronounced intentionally their name did the word Philistines turn into Palestinians. Some say the original Philistines were Cretes who crated up and moved from Crete.

The Palestinians say the Jews showed up much later when many who followed enslaved relatives into Egypt were kicked out for illegal immigration. Evidently the word got back to Jerusalem that being a slave in Egypt was more enjoyable than being a free man in Palestine. They point to Isiah 11: 14, 15 as proof that Philistia predated Judea. Judea is the name the Romans call the area around Jerusalem. Did the Romans give the Jews their name? That's how poor the Jews were. They didn't have a name until the Roman legions showed up.

The Palestinians call the area around Jerusalem Palestine. The name game is another example of how little there is to do and talk about in Jerusalem. So "Who's on first?" And there is no one who wants to be called second. It all settled down after a time. The Palestinians and the Jews lived together in relative peace. But then the Babylonians invaded and took Jewish slaves for their building projects in Baghdad. Some accounts of that Babylonian raid have Jews begging to be taken back to Baghdad. Many of them were in Egypt illegally and can't stand being back in Palestine or Judea or is it Israel?

Then came the Persians and the Romans who wanted slaves and taxes. Jews and Palestinians would wait on corners to be rounded up for rendition to Persia or Rome. Palestine is a place that many are from and many don't want to go back to. There are many who would prefer to leave but don't have a destination. But the Roman's presence has subtly offered an escape route. Empire building needs taxable real estate and populations who can be enslaved or occupied. So it follows that Romans laid down roads during their conquests. The roads went to far away places. But the roads also lead back to Rome. The challenge is to get to Rome or other parts of the Roman Empire and get out of Jerusalem and stop telling lies to compensate for a meager existence.

The place is the Sea of Galilee. It's early afternoon. It's hot and the sky is clear. The water is calm. The shore birds are flying about. It's peaceful. There's a young man with a light beard and long hair on the beach. His clothes suggest that he modified a common robe. That's a real fashion statement. Immediately this man has credibility. The robe has become a tunic. It's cut short to knee length and the upper portion has short sleeves and a light weight belt to keep it all in

place. He is handsome and has excellent facial structure that makes itself known in spite of the fine-hair,
light beard. The features are both symmetrical and refined. This man really stands out. He doesn't look like
a Jew or Palestinian — lucky him. He is surrounded
by a few men and women. Women fell in love with him
before he spoke. His looks are magnetic. The women
just unashamedly stare. Some of their husbands or
boyfriends ask questions. He's speaking to them in a
somewhat formal way despite the informality of the
setting. It's Jesus.

Two fishermen are coming to shore in a boat with
their catch. If Jesus is the top, the fishermen are the
bottom. They are Peter and John. They have been
friends and have been fishing these waters for most of
their lives. They know what the other will say before
he says it. Sometimes they will prompt each other to
say what they said yesterday about the same subject
with the same comment they spoke a year earlier. They
are middle aged and weathered looking. They show
the effects of more weather patterns on their face than
Palestine gets in a year. They fish because they know
nothing else. They are not happy with prospects of being fishermen till they die. But they are keen. Peter is
particularly analytic and greedy. He is also bitter.

Peter says, "Isn't that Mary's son Jesus? It looks like he's holding a gathering of his court."

John remarks, "Yeah. He likes to speak about issues both political and religious. His topics are all about equality. He says everyone should either help others or be helped by others. You would think he's running for office. Politics and religion, it's like talking about the weather. It ain't going to change by just talking. But interestingly there is a definite light heart influence about his message. He's entertaining to listen to. That's what makes him an engaging fellow. He's a dreamer and outspoken. He tells any one who will listen to trust in God. God will provide or is it nature will provide? He uses them interchangeably. He instructs that we just have to adjust our demands to pursue a middle course between greed and poverty.

He claims equality for all as the path to the middle way. He drinks some. Don't we all? Mary really spoiled him. He never had to work. She bought him the best clothes she could afford, hired a tutor and home schooled him in eastern philosophies together with the traditional subjects. I think he took off on his own for many years. I heard he went to India. His mothers choice of schooling wet his appetite. He never learned how to behave with children his own age. I think she feels guilty some how. Sometimes he gets in a dark brooding mood. Something is bugging him."

Peter pursues," I can guess what's bugging him. It's the same thing that's bugging me. He's bored with Jerusalem. He's bored being a Jew. Why did he come back from India? If I had done what he did, I would have stayed in India. I didn't seize the opportunity to travel when I was younger. So life has passed me by. It's my fault. I could have been somebody. I could have left my father and mother and my brother. They could have gotten by in the fishing business without me. But I was set in my ways early on. My parents always drilled me on the importance of the family. One for all and all for one. Stick that jingo you know where. That's fine if you are a drone. But what if you have some talent? Why should one sacrifice his life for people who might not be as loyal to you as they want you to be to them?

John my friend we are born to migrate. But thousands of years of civilization, and I use the term loosely around this place has killed the wanderlust in many. The spirit of adventure is kaput. Only a lack of courage keeps me in this hell hole. Also my looks. I make no excuses. My face is ugly. All its parts look like hand-me-downs from different relatives. There's no symmetry and the skin is of poor quality. The hair is a tangled-wire mess. The hair and the skin are great for weathering the blistering heat, but polite society wants nothing to do with me. I have some education. I could speak well and tell entertaining stories. I like people. I could be of service. I want more friends. I would like to leave a mark on this earth. I would like to be remembered. I have no children. Time is running out. But no one wants to be seen with me. No one wants to be seen with me unless they are buying fish. So I fish. I'm up early. No one sees me. I catch fish who hate me. And then I go home and prepare for the next day. I'm sick of it. Sorry, John for running off like that. But it wells up and then I have to vent or I will explode. I would drink more if I could afford it. I would have a girl friend but where might she be? Where did Mary get exposed to these cosmopolitan and urbane child rearing techniques?"

John answers, "She has led a full life. If you take my meaning. She was a favorite of the well traveled Romans who routinely get short stays in Jerusalem. They naturally want to impress the local talent with a view to bedding them. So they talk of their adventures and the exotic places they have lived. They brag of the women they have known and the sexual techniques they have mastered. None of the women get up and leave. Then a little wine, a little atmosphere, a little more conversation and voila! This is time tested foreplay. Chalk up another conquest.

We can't do that. The gals know that we have no stories or techniques. We have no shiny Roman uniforms. We can't strut because we don't have anything to strut about. And we don't have loose coins to spend. We exist from day to day. Try smiling with that regimen to look forward to. I also wish I could afford to drink heavily. Now you got me feeling sorry for myself. My early childhood experiences with my family are similar. My mother and father were a couple of dull dogs. It would have been different if I thought they meant well, but that would require more exertion then they were willing or capable of. It's this country Peter. To live here one has to surrender to humdrum. One has to surrender to slim pickings. After thousands of years one's face tells the whole sad story of Jerusalem and its environs. We have to invent this God who supposedly cares about us. Gee I wonder what the differences would be if he didn't care for us? The lucky ones were the Jews who escaped the Exodus. They got to stay in Egypt. They are valued members of wealthy Egyptian society. I've got a relative in

Thebes who I correspond with from time to time. He sends me some money. He writes about how lush life is there. He is a majordomo. He bathes daily and has an Egyptian wife and two sons who work a tract of land as sharecroppers. They have a retirement plan and are on good terms with the master who is an engineer for pharaoh."

Peter answers, "What do you mean 'Jews who escaped the Exodus'?"

"Contrary to the holy scriptures, all the Jews in Egypt did not escape. Actually, only some were kicked out. Originally the Egyptians enslaved Jews for the building projects of the pharaohs. The enslaved Jews wrote home about how lucky they were to get out of Palestine, so their relatives started to trickle into Egypt. The trickle became a flood. Eventually the Egyptians had a massive illegal immigration problem. Some of the illegals talked up the advantages of labor unions. Some advocated the right to vote for all. The more extreme suggested that parts of Egypt were promised to the Israelis by their God. Their was also some speculation that Ramses II had a Jewish mother. That was the last straw. That's when the round up happened and the forced deportation of illegal Jews commenced. I've got a distantly related aunt in Babylon who is a descendant of my mothers side of the family. Her family ended up in Babylon after a raid many years ago on Jerusalem. She is a scribe in the bureau of land affairs in Mesopotamia. She has a wonderful connection to major private land owners who need help with state subsidies So she helps with the paper work and gets perqs of marvelous food choices. Lucky are the diaspora."

Peter remarks, "That's interesting. Getting back to Mary, so she picked up ideas for raising Jesus in pillow talk. Not bad for an afternoon's rapture. Sex, wine and free advice on how to raise a child to be a cosmopolitan. I kind of like Jesus. I've seen him around and heard him speak. He thinks he has something to say. That tutoring and far east travel experience show up in his speech and mannerisms. He feels comfortable and relaxed. That comes from broadening your outlook. But you say there's something wrong with him?"

John answers,"Yeah, he doesn't take the demands of life seriously. He speaks of this wise middle way, as if that's all he needs to say since it's self-explanatory and people will know what he is talking about. And he paradoxically speaks about giving to receive. He also says work is fine but too much work is bad. It's not that he's lazy. I think he just doesn't want to be bothered with the repetition of a day job or its this middle way advice.

His traveling has jaded him to routine. He advises that constant work leads to greed. It's an involuntary, subtle habit that grows like a sickness which accustoms people to work for work's sake and then to pile up money for money's sake. Then one is lost to the beauty and charm of the natural world. Also God is forgotten. But he also cautions about being too withdrawn from society. He warns people of being to much of an ascetic or resorting to begging for alms. It sounds like he has lived through both polar life styles and speaks with the authority of experience. He philosophizes in a stream of conscious manner to any one who will listen. Yet there is something deeply personal that is gnawing in him."

Peter asks, "He mentioned God? So he believes in God. None of that for me. I gave up on God a long ago. He went when the tooth fairy stopped giving me a coin for the teeth that I lost while growing up. So maybe he came back to do Gods work? All that wonderful travel experience wasted in pursuit of Gods work? I'll never understand people who try to please God. Consider this John. Here's this almighty deity who keeps track of us mortals. He wants to keep count on our offerings. What kind of almighty needs stinking pieces of fish offered irregularly by smelly followers? I don't like my life. Why should God be interested in my life? Doesn't he have anything better to do? There is no God. There are only men who invent him so they can run a business enterprise without sweating one drop. Ever meet a rabbi who wasn't a phony? I never have. And I'm not waiting to finally meet one. I left religion long ago. They extend their hand in greeting but immediately are reaching for your purse. There I go running off at the mouth again. John, do you think there's a connection between Mary's guilt feelings and the something that's bothering Jesus?"

"Could be. I think that Jesus is suspect about Joseph. Jesus has this idea that Joseph isn't his father. But Jesus also talks passionately about the poor and the need for all to share because God will provide to those who are charitable. Give things away and things will be given to you. Maybe that's what gnawing at him?"

Peter says, "Boy you said a mouthful. Are you sure you heard Jesus correctly? It doesn't make sense. 'God will provide to people who give things away.' And yet there is a bit of wisdom there if your ear is trained for subtly. "

"Peter, what I said was close to what he said. I

didn't get it either. But Jesus has an instinct for spotting developing social trends. He's hip to what the people need but feels frustrated that he can't do more for the poor. I think he's got too much time on his hands. I've never seen him sweat at a job. He's a born speaker. God knows where he got those ideas."

"And what makes Jesus suspect Joseph is not his real father?"

"Next time you see Joseph, think and compare Jesus to him. They couldn't be more different. Joseph is short, almost squat, dark with thick features and thick, black, wire-like hair. But Jesus is light skinned, with light, fine hair, refined features and he is tall. Joseph barely makes it to his chin. And then it really gets worse when Joseph opens his mouth. If Jesus is cosmopolitan, then by comparison Joseph never left the crib. Another suspicious fact is, I swear that Mary introduced me to Joseph many years ago before Jesus was born. Then she said that he was her cousin. Well, some years later Joseph moves in. Mary then says that Joseph is her new husband. And then some months later Jesus is born. They were expecting a girl, but the boy child Jesus shows up. He cuts more of a noticeable figure than a girl would have. So he's noticed. I think Mary's over indulgence toward Jesus relates in some way to the question of Jesus' father. Whoever that may be? She feels ashamed. It's like she feels that everyone thinks, ' Where did this kid come from?'"

Peter picks up, "Mary did drink some. I guess she cant drink much before it gets her in an amorous mood. She has a great figure. Oh boy, I've seen her a little tipsy in the middle of the day. Didn't she have some affairs with the Romans?"

"Yeah. The Romans have imported wines. Not our cheap Jew stuff. Mary acquired a taste for it. And she didn't mind a barter for a rapture in the afternoon with the guy. One in particular was this smooth talking, fine featured, light skinned with light, fine hair and tall Roman officer from Calabria up in Italy. I think his name was Don Giovanni."

Peter suggests, "Jesus has something to brood about if the paternity question is bothering him. But the fact is he's got Greek-God looks. Who would rather have a legitimate father's ugly looks when one has matinee idol features, albeit from an escapade on the wrong side of the sheets? Let's go listen to what Jesus is talking about to that group. But first let's get these fish out of the sun and treat them with salt. Salt is so expensive. I'm so tired of this fish business. I'm middle aged and I'm getting worried that the rest of my life will resemble today. More dead fish until I am as dead as they are. I hope not."

John pops, "I cut my salt with some sand. This tilapia's eye reminds me of my wife. She's always got one eye on me. And her eye is about as cold as this dead fish. Arranged marriages are so old fashion. They should be discontinued. But there's a lot of money in matchmaking. It's a side business for the money grubbing rabbis, but the poor arranged participants suffer a fate worse than death. Look at me and my wife Gevelta. She's like sleeping with a dead fish."

"Were there ever good times with Gevelta? "

John thought and John thought and then John thought some more. Then John scratched his head and thought.

Peter shook his head sympathetically and added, "Hey that's a good idea about the sand."

The two fishermen secured their boat. They cleaned and processed the fish with salt and wrapped them. They then headed out to where Jesus was speaking. By now there is a larger gathering. More men and women are listening intently. They are mostly young. Peter wonders why they aren't working. John and Peter stand at the back of the group.

Jesus notices the two and continues speaking,

"Therefore do not be anxious saying what shall we eat? Or what shall we drink? What are we to put on? For your father knows that you need all these things. But seek first the kingdom of God and his justice and all these things will be given to you besides. Therefore do not be anxious about tomorrow for tomorrow will have anxieties of its own. Sufficient for the day is its own trouble."

Jesus' voice trails off. He holds out his arms spontaneously. The people are moved. They are also speechless. Neither they or Peter or John has never heard this kind of religious pitch. It didn't make sense. *'Seek first the kingdom of God . . . and all things will be given you'.* Something for nothing never makes sense. But it wasn't the words that were credible. It was the personal, good looking, convincing speaking style of Jesus that moved the people. The words were swallowed in whole. Some of the crowd timidly approached Jesus to touch him. Some wanted to shake his hand. Some wanted to hug him. Some had tears well up in their eyes. It was a genuinely moving experience. Even the old salts Peter and John are somewhat shaken. The crowd drifts away, but doesn't go very far. They break down into their original parts. They sit and talk and marvel over the words of promise.

Peter speaks out, "That was a moving sermon.

'What me worry?' was the message. But what really came across was the persona of Jesus. I'll bet if you ask those same people tomorrow what Jesus spoke about at least half wouldn't recall. But all would be able to describe Jesus' physical looks and his way of speaking in detail. That's star quality."

Jesus is now on his knees in the sand. He's facing the sun. The warmth of the rays bring a smile to his face. His eyes are closed and he's enjoying a peaceful repose. He acts like a capricious child who enjoys self expression. He is delighting in the after glow of his well received talk.

John speaks, "We enjoyed your talk."

Jesus finally opens his eyes and speaks quietly but with a slight petulance about being brought back to earth from his high." Thank you. What are your names?"

"I'm John. I fish these waters along with my friend Peter here. We know your mother and father."

"You think that I'm drunk. I am not. I don't drink any more. Have you two ever felt care free? I feel care-free now. How long will it last I don't know. Have you ever tried soma?"

John screws up his face. "Soma? What's that?"

Jesus explains, "I tried it in India. I ran across

it when I was seeking knowledge of other religions. The religion and God of Abraham and Moses is more about weights and measures. How much is owed and how are you going to pay for it? It's too righteous with a mercantile goal.

But Buddhism is on the right track. It points to a sustainable living experience. It's about facing reality with equilibrium. Maintaining balance no matter what the head winds. Being satisfied with life as it comes. I studied Buddhism and Hinduism. There's no thought in the west that hasn't been thought first in the east. Maybe because the sun rises in the east, they have been at work longer than the people in the west. A few hours multiplied by the millennium add up.

Some holy men arrived at their religion by using soma. Then they don't want it anymore. That's my experience. It permanently expanded my mind and I don't use it anymore. It's the plant of the Gods. You can chew the leaf or you can put the powdered form in liquid. It helps one to see clearly. It transports me out of this humdrum. It deconstructs my every day experience to the very doors of perception. It breaks the spell of the drone of reality by showing what precedes reality. Do you understand what I am talking about? It's about my interface with the world at the most basic level. First there's me, then there's the a experience of reality- sights,sounds and taste. It really intensifies the living experience. If all you two guys do is fish then you should try some soma. Do yourselves a favor. It's a cheap trip. I haven't seen my Indian friend recently. I'll let you know when he's in town. He has got the goods.

I have a friend. His name is John the Baptist. He never took soma and he's never been to India. But he got to the place where soma experimenters wanted to go. He did it naturally. He doesn't worry about anything. His is truly inspiring and has a comforting philosophy. He lives by a river outside of town. He baptizes people. He simply dunks them in water and instructs them to live a simple loving life. Just roll with life. Surf life's waves. It will all balance out. The cold water is a shock of awakening. Buddha's name means awakening. Living in the country sharpens the senses. Soma sharpens senses artificially. "

John looks at a loss after hearing Jesus recite this non stop stream of consciousness revelation. It's bewildering. It's as if Jesus is the loneliest person on earth and he's dying to make contact with some one.

John says," No. I have never heard of soma. But it sounds interesting. Maybe I'll get some for Gevelta and me. It couldn't hurt our outlooks. Would you like some water?"

Jesus becomes impatient. "Thanks. I'll have a sip." He then gets up and walks off.

Peter blurts, "He's a happy caring rogue. His gray eyes look directly at you. I wonder if that Calabrese father speculation is correct. I've never seen a southern Italian with gray eyes. Those eye colors are mostly from Germany. Of course, the Germans do get around and that includes destinations like Calabria. Jesus is a natural entertainer. He's an exhibitionist. I enjoy the confidence in his voice. He's so sure of himself. But his voice has no trace of being preachy. It's a unique voice that can count to ten and make it sound like the first time it was ever done by anyone anywhere. He's also got these great looks to go along with the tall athletic build. He could go to places that we couldn't. People see us coming in a Philistine or an up-scale neighborhood and they lock the doors and unlock the kennels to let the dogs out.

One day I saw him by that old abandoned Babylonian warehouse that some rabbis claim for their temple. In an uncharacteristically loud voice, he was complaining and haranguing passersby about how badly many people in Jerusalem were doing. They didn't have enough food. They lived in run down and crowded housing. And there wasn't enough good paying jobs to go around. He even challenged business owners and known charitable supporters that they weren't doing enough for the street people. Jesus is somewhat spoiled. You're right about that. He gives free rein to his mercurial mood swings. But his tunic is dirty. I could smell it over the odor of my fishing clothes. If he wants to go to the next level, he'll have to clean up. Just a few things would make this kid pass for a patrician."

John comments, "There's been talk about his some what seditious talks. Telling people that they have inalienable rights when they are born really rankles the ruling class in Jerusalem. Some of the local rabbis and merchants resent his stirring up the street people. Jesus implies the street people are equal to the rich and powerful. But only because others have many desirable things and wealth already that there is none for them. So they will be constantly denied equality because of a scarcity. He's driving a wedge between people. The rabbis call him a democrat. They accuse him of introducing democracy via a Trojan Horse of religion. They are deathly afraid of his philosophy and have gone to Pontius Pilate with their concerns."

Peter corrects, "I don't think that's what he's really

saying, but it's close. I'm not sure either. He will cause tongues to wag and he will get blow back from vested interests. I believe Jesus is a good person. He's honest. He's got a touch of dilettante, but he wont reach a mass market alone. That's where we come in. We could develop a public image and public following. Put him in the proper venue with the right kind of direction and we could make a bundle. He could be our ticket out of this place. There's no one like Jesus for natural charisma. I believe he thinks God and nature are the same and if you trust in both all will be resolved happily and without a sweat. That day I saw him downtown and heard him speaking he said something to the effect that ' . . . *look at the birds of the air, they do not sow or reap or gather into barns yet their heavenly father provides all they need . . .* ' That kind of thinking doesn't make sense, yet I believe he is sincere when he makes such a cock-eyed statements. Obviously his premise is wrong. Reality says people must work. Jesus says in God we trust. But the actual motivation for all living things is 'In growth we trust or in power we trust'. It's about the will to power and the will to survive. Living beings waiting for God to provide would have perished long ago. But people don't think things through. Most people would rather do anything but think. It will be easy for them to blur the message of Jesus, particularly if we help them. We will massage his message to put blame on the wealthy for the shortfalls of the poor.

The rabbis are right. He is a democrat. We will develop a religion around his words. It will include brick and mortar churches that we will own. Our goal will be to harness the discontent of the relatively poor. We will roll over opposition if we can get up to a critical mass of recognition and followers. We have to make a maximum effort very quickly before they try to shut us down. And they will try to shut us down. The cozy positions of wealth and power will be directly threatened by Jesus and us. I'll bet the Roman governor Pontius Pilate has got an ear full about Jesus already. Pilate wants to please the local merchants. They want something from the Roman occupiers to offset the taxes and loss of control. That will pale in comparison to the earfuls Pilate will get if we get momentum. It will be like a brush fire that roars into a forest fire. Nobody wants a democrat screaming religious entitlements of equality. Not even their God will help them when we unleash the power of the mobs who are not equipped with critical thinking.

Any of his shortcomings are totally eclipsed by

his strong points. He's a lotus springing from the mud. He's really good looking. He doesn't look like us. Also, that credible, shameless, naïve, cock-sure spread-the-happiness-philosophy delivered in a singular speaking voice tone is engaging. Sounds like you are correct about your guess that he never held a job. Oh, these liberals want to pass out things that don't belong to them. But he's got star quality. Loud mouths have an eternal charm. They are cheap entertainment. They talk so much that sooner or later they say something interesting. It's as if they could be just parroting, but the really good loud mouth says things in such a way that's as if its the first time the idea has ever been presented. Particularly with his dramatic looks. The beard has got to go. His facial construction is one in a million. It's got to be show cased. And the hair has to be shortened to frame the face. We are talking about trifles. He's almost perfect right now. The gals will fall in love. You noticed them almost dropped jaw and drip drooling at the gathering.

No women has ever done that because of me, not even in those dark caves that I would choose to have a rendezvous. They couldn't see me yet I still felt some resistance. The men will notice and try to be like him. He will attract people. I don't know how long he will last. He could pass for a northern white. He should wash daily and clean his clothes. He really needs some new clothes. We could tailor them and together with his new facial look we could start a new fashion style. Remember John, we have to think big. We will have one crack at this opportunity. If the fashions catch on here we could take it directly to Rome. There's plenty of clothiers who might be interested in what's new in fashion in the Roman provinces. We could develop a new look for today's youth. A new line of clothing could make us rich. I have to get a piece of him. He would do better with a manager and a producer to line up sermons along with some light entertainment. We can smooth his rough edges. He shouldn't give the advice or anecdotes for free. It has to be presented in a serious, dramatic fashion to set up credibility with the audience. It will be somewhat of an outdoor symposium, which will be very classy in tone.

But we have to tweak his message. It's not going to be that God or nature will provide. The people would love to believe that but they are not that stupid. So we will blur nature and God with an addition of the wealthy and the central government. That will shame money and power into supporting the under served. The new message will be that the wealthy owe some of what they have to others less fortunate. That's nothing new. It's what democracies are all about. But democracy brought down Greece. That's why the Romans came up with the republic as a governing model. That's about peer to peer government patricians governing plebeians and all the bureaucracies in between. But that can't last either. Because in the end it always defaults to 'one man, one vote'. And that's were we get them. Its like the dice game. We have seven on our side most of the time. Our seven is indiscriminate population growth. And that always ends up in chaos. We ride this wave as long as we can. When Jesus articulates and points his finger of shame and guilt at the wealthy and what they owe to the poor, it will sound like the first time any one has ever said it. We will get Jesus to sell guilt as a mass market product, which only the wealthy can afford to buy it. It will put their abundance in a negative light to the poor. That will rattle their cage. We will make them embarrassed. We will accuse the wealthy of mean spirited critical thinking. We will carve out discrimination as a dirty word. But things can be put right if the haves agree to share some of their assets with the have nots."

John interrupts, "Sell guilt? We don't own guilt. How can we sell something we don't own ? What do you mean by that?"

"We don't have to own something to sell it. Look at the Romans who say they are the masters of the world. In fact they are not, but they have an army that acts like they are. Consequently they have credibility. It's not who or what you are, it's what you say you are and then back it up with military power. Or in our case we will non-violently train our masters to feel guilty. It's like a dripping pipe on someone's forehead. It's a politically correct alternative to personal greed. We have nothing to lose. The wealthy who have inherited money will be the first to cave in. They didn't earn the money so they don't know about hard work.

The people who actually work for their wealth will be harder to move philosophically. We could make it easier for them by rewarding their charity work with positions in our church or certifying a place in heaven when they die. People would rather go along to get along. It's simple. I just told you. Here it is again. Jesus preaches trust in God and all will be well. We will add that the wealthy and the powerful in government should help also. Jesus will be selling democracy in a religious package. And here is where we come in. We provide a venue and sell tickets to those that want to hear how to get what rightfully belongs to them. We

will try to hook his messianic message to a secular revolution against the present day government. We will
upend the prevailing philosophy of power which is
based on merit and heredity and change it to celebrate
people without a noble birth and people who's families
are poor. We have time and population numbers on are
side. The more people born the more our ranks of politics grows.

If we can get this idea off the ground, we would be
unstoppable. We could create a serious forum for his
presentations. I'll direct that. You, John, will handle
the food and entertainment. Maybe you could offer
fish at retail prices at some of our produced gatherings? Next time I see him, I will tell him our thoughts.
You want in John? We'll keep the books also."

"Why don't you ask me if I've got a better idea?
Ask me if I want to smell like fish for the rest of my
life? Ask me if I want to hear Gevelta's question every
night until the day I die?"

"What does she ask you?"

"Where's the beef?" John continues, "But I'm not
putting any shekels up. I'm still short because of that
last brainstorm you had."

"What brainstorm was that?"

"It was the time that you had an idea for selling

off our old fishing nets with that marketing pitch you dreamed up. I spent quite a few shekels on posters, many of which I still possess, advertising 'Ties That Bind Nets". And that lay away plan with only a portion of fishermen income to tithe them to the contract. Peter you got to remember that contracts need enforcers and we Jews aren't up to busting faces and the shyster advocates are so expensive."

"You're getting to be more of an old lady everyday day. We don't have to put up money. Jesus will work for nothing. And we can bring our unsold fish to the gigs and get cash from the audience. Hey, we wont even salt them."

John perks up, "I never thought of that. Boy, when you do the right thing everything falls into place. I'm in Peter."

Peter remarks poignantly, "His strengths are his good looks and his passionate out reach to help people with that naïve God-will-provide and I quote, *'Ask and it shall be given to you seek and you shall find and knock and the door will be open to you'* pitch. People will want to believe that. They will substitute the word 'work' with a more desirable 'collection' of debt that is owed them. They will figure it out quick that there's more of them than those with wealth. So why not make it happen with force or without force? That's nothing new to us Jews. We always claim discrimination. It's a way of embarrassing people into letting us into their societies. We look different. But Jesus doesn't look like you and me. He can say the same things we been saying, but with his looks and passion, people will believe, try to help and want to be a part. He's almost Messianic. He doesn't realize how angry he'll make the wealthy. They won't go without a fight. Jesus may lose his life, but the siren call to all those poor that they are "entitled" will be irresistible. Ka-ching ka-ching. I can hear the shekels dropping in already."

John speculates, "Don't worry. We make ours up front. If they come after him, we bail. Should we post disclaimers at the gatherings making the point that the views of our acts do not necessarily reflect management? That's all the boiler plate we need. If the government pressures us we can push back. My wife's brother is a shyster who has incriminating paintings and depositions on a lot of the local officials, including some of the Roman occupiers. If push comes to shove we could threaten to post the paintings on some of our old posters. You know go public. They can have Jesus, but they can't have us without an embarrassing fight. Hey, then I could get rid of the posters I've stored for years. This is really symmetrical when you are in the right deal. Everything falls into place. Peter, we're bigger than Tiberius and the Roman Senate."

"You are correct. We have the potential to bring the whole Roman Empire down. We have to make it clear that our relationship with Jesus is only business. We are agnostic when it comes to religion or politics. Why John, I could almost whistle a tune. But hey, why entertain someone else for free? From now on no more mister fish monger. No body will stand in our way. Maybe we should lobby the Pontius Pilate court. Offer free tickets and free fish if he and his operatives allow us the usage of that Roman amphitheater. Those bacchanal stage acts that Pilate promotes are sublime. Maybe we get a warm up act for Jesus. What do you think?"

"You mean like belly dancers? My relation in Egypt could help me. I could get a letter off to him today."

"No. The gals are too expensive. The people would resent Jesus interrupting the acts when he came on stage. We need some comedy. Maybe some black face to do a send up of the Nubians along with some singing? My cousin Jol has a son who could do all of that. Maybe a little social comment jokes by Mort who is

Saul's son. How about he triangulates the Romans and the Egyptians and the Philistines. Maybe we come up with real estate for free. Then we get naming rights and sell shares and oh my mind is just flooded with clever ideas. With that kind of power we could rewrite history."

"Clever yes. But are they wise ideas Peter? You are talking about a lot of rearrangement. Relax. We don't know if Jesus will go for it."

"Oh, he'll go for it. What are a great voice and good looks and a bratty ego good for if you can't strut and talk bombastically to a few thousand people now and again. And get paid as a bonus? He won't refuse. Scriptures promise a Messiah. Well, Peter and John proudly present right here, right now, on this stage —The Messiah. Herrrrrrre's Jesus!!!!!! That's an angle he might warm up to?"

"Pay. Did you say pay? How much and why?"

"We have to give him something. Don't we? Something small don't you think ?"

"Well I always say when it comes to money matters, particularly when I'm trying to get a bill reduced, ' Man does not live by bread alone'. I think I heard Jesus say that once. How about we say the immediate income from our ticket sales, endorsements, fish sales etc will be needed for a building fund so there won't be any salary for him right away?"

"Right. A building fund. That's what we'll do."

"We'll build a meeting place. Let's start looking for some more derelict Babylonian warehouses like the rabbis have. That will be our theater. It will host entertainment and weekly religious meetings. We will put on readings of the teachings of Jesus. Occasionally we will invite a guest witness of his or her encounter with Jesus. You know, some oral history. We'll knock out the down town rabbis with Jesus the Messiah and his new church. Over night the rabbis will become re-dundant. They won't like it. All that trading business that goes on in the old warehouse they call a temple will dry up. The live animals for slaughter, memori-al trinkets and the highest margin product of them all — simony. The Samaritan sorcerer Simon Magus came up with that con. He offered church position franchise and or heavenly access for money. Simony comes from his name. Basically we'll be the low cost producer of religion on a mass scale. We won't pray for help. We will demand help or there will be hell to pay."

Peter says, "Correct me if I'm wrong or leave something out. We'll market Jesus as the Messiah. His message is simple. Trust in God he will provide. We blur that message to include the wealthy as a backup to God if the almighty doesn't provide enough soon enough. All that is needed is the price of admission to his sermons and a little left over to buy unsalted fish. We will be the management team and the producers who make way for Jesus to expound his empowerment philosophy to all. People will go for this hook, line and sinker. And no matter what happens to Jesus, we will have a hall to show for our efforts. You know, this guy could be as big for us dead as he is alive. Legends of dead founders sell tickets. Plus we can revise his life to include miracles and visitations from the paranormal. Martyred founders sell even more tickets. We could put it all in a book. Then we could sell the book. We will be in control of his trade marked message and we retain full rights actual or implied."

"Peter, that's a cold statement about a possible martyrs death. But that's pretty much it. I like that religion idea. Then no one can say any of us are greedy. Jesus claims the glory and the intangibles while we collect here and now. Boy do I like those margins."

"It would be better if he could lighten up a bit. Add humor and he will attract bigger crowds. These people don't want to be preached to. They know their faults and problems. The honest ones know that they

are worthless. Others don't like a regular life and prefer the street and a feral living style. They just want
a couple of hours of cheap entertainment. The philosophy and religious instruction can be couched in
situation parables. Then you get 'em with their guard
down. Then it will sink in. Then they'll come back for
more. His philosophy will rub rough on many people
with wealth and power. He will have to learn when
to back down and not take himself so seriously. The
ground is filled with people who forgot that they were
mere mortals and that they could possibly be wrong in
some cases. And there's a time for diplomacy. Live to
fight another day." Peter says.

John quickly adds, "Ask him if he can sing. The
next best thing to humorous stories is a warm ballad."

"Good question. Will do."

Chapter III

Peter Meets Jesus and John the Baptist

bout a week later, Peter is in Jerusalem. It's the capitol of Palestine. Different demographic sections make up the city. Philistines, Jews, bedouins, Roman occupiers and ex patriots from around the Mediterranean live and do business. The first and lasting impression of the city is that everywhere there is dust. It's a normal dry hot day with most people in doors. Only thirsty dogs or tourists are out in the midday sun. But Peter spots Jesus with another man. They are leaning up against a building in the shade.

"Hi Jesus, remember me? I'm Peter. John and I saw you on the beach about a week ago."

Jesus answers in a short annoyed tone, "Yes."

Peter deflects the snub by going on the offensive with a question about Jesus' friend. The implication is, two can play this insult game and here's my example. If you don't take me seriously then the next example will be directly at you.

The friend is John the Baptist. John is clothed, and that's a generous description, in what's left of a camel hair garment that when new would still be considered unfinished and of poor quality. The only other stitch of clothing on this bare foot, tangled haired, dirty faced, bearded man with some food clinging to the beard in an almost festooned fashion, is a filthy leather loin wrap. But what he doesn't have on serves to showcase what he does have to show. His physique is classic. He's above average height. And the bulges are all in the right places and impressive in size. Some of the gals love him for his cave man presence. All types of women slum with him in the river.

Peter asks Jesus, "Who's this?"

Jesus senses the pique in Peter's question, "This is John the Baptist. He baptized me in the river last month. He's the most original and well balanced person I know."

"Oh. Only a month ago. How can anyone get that dirty in only a month. You guys dating much? Do your gals spot you by sense of smell or is it the other way around? What's in your beard John? It looks body parts of locusts held together by honey."

The Baptist only barely smiles. He shows his chipped and dirty teeth as a sign of a no contest response to Peter's accurate assessment."

But Jesus intervenes, "What gives you the right to insult my friend? He's worth fifty of your kind."

"Since when is telling the truth an insult?"

Jesus asks haughtily, "Is there a reason why I should continue to talk to you? You don't look like much of catch. I don't know if there's more hair coming out of your nose or coming out of your ears. Because the hanging hair gardens of your eyebrows get in the way. And do you know the difference between the smell of your wife and the fish you clean? Or is all the same now? At least John here started his baptism shtick to clean up the women before he rammed home his heartfelt message. I've met some of the foxiest gals around these parts at John's bend in the river. And they all strip so willingly and prefer to stay a while. And for that moment every part of John and his new friends are so clean. But the take away from their awakening splash is they are never the same again. It's a spiritual and physical awakening."

Peter's face relaxes. Jesus has outed him, "You speak the truth. I am ugly. But you are handsome and in general very striking in appearance. People want to hear what you have to say before you open your mouth to speak. But when you speak it gets even better. I need you. You can go places I can't go. You can say things that people will listen to and believe. I can't do any of that. But I've got things to trade in return. I can manage you to maximize your potential. I will marquee you so that a great deal more people will show up when you show up. At first it will be mostly barter. I haven't got much cash. Did you want to listen to my offer?"

Jesus is delighted that he verbally gutted Peter. He says, "And what about an apology to my friend John?"

"How about I offer him a proposition also?"

John jumps in, "What kind of offer?"

"John, you are going to be the 'before.' And after I get through with Jesus he will be the 'after.' It will be a simple demonstration. You won't get much for your appearances. But you won't starve and it beats racing the birds to the locust or getting elbowed or worse by bears after the honey. But I promise once you are exposed on the stage you will need an appointment secretary to book all your 'baptisms.' But we will charge a small fee for your 'baptisms' which I get one-third of and you keep the balance."

The baptists face screws down to the visage of a calculating accountant. He answers, "I'll do it on a trial basis."

Jesus is curious, "Peter, perhaps you had better more fully explain what you want of me and what you will do for me."

"Jesus, you have special appeal. For whatever reason, you don't look like a Jew. You could pass for a patrician. Your physical looks, your way of speaking and your philosophy make you unique. I want to give you a make over. We'll shorten your hair, shave your beard and clean up your garments and get you some new ones. Your fine features will be the first draw to people. You have a sincere and engaging way of speaking, that's your second draw. And thirdly, your philosophy of trust in God will draw thousands. You will make people feel better about themselves. They will come to expect that things will be provided for them simply by asking. I can help you tweak your message to that purpose. Many have tried to teach the philosophy you speak. But they can't pull it off. But you have the looks. You have a velvet articulation cadence of speaking. And most importantly you believe in your message. That comes through loud and clear. In short you are magnetic. I think I can make you come off as a great philosopher and teacher. What do you think?"

Jesus is uncharacteristically at a loss for words, "How about wow? Where would I speak? Who would come? What's your take?"

"John is my partner. We will produce the shows and make all necessary arrangements. Tickets and food will be sold at the venues. John and I will handle that. Any permission that is necessary from the Roman occupiers to hold these events will go through our production team."

"And what's my share look like? I don't have a taste for locusts," asks Jesus.

"Well to begin, you will have to make do with our support and a small stipend. But clothing, coaching and help with your scripts will be provided by John and I. We are going to take you from a voice in the desert to a force that will be heard in Rome. You're going to the next level. It's rarefied but you can handle it. Are you in?"

"So a fisherman tells me that I need a couple of fishermen to put my message across? Isn't that a cold splash of water in the face? Mom didn't prepare me for this." Jesus replies in a humble fashion.

"You could always go back to the river with John here. But with my offer, you may get the people to form a river and come to you."

That clinched it, "OK Peter. I'm in. John comes along also. But I insist that I'll write my own material. I'm going to continue to be honest with my followers. You and your partner will provide my personal make over and be the producers. But I'm not going to be "Country "J" and The Fish."

"You are smarter than I thought. You pocketed your arrogance and threw in with two fishermen. For my part I will match that gesture. From now on my partner and I will present you to the public as the Messiah. We will address you in an appropriate fashion and promote others to recognize you as the savior. I will be in touch. Now I go to make the arrangements for your immediate makeover. We're going to make you the Messiah."

"The Messiah? I'm not the Messiah. I studied eastern religions because I felt that the laws of Abraham and Moses lacked a comforting message that people needed. Moses was about "don'ts". There was no joy in his message. I want to be proactive in comforting people. My philosophy is about promoting love and doing good works and sharing with people in need and living in harmony with nature. If we steward the land respectively the land will take care of us. Trust in

God and trust in nature. Be prudent and not greedy."

Peter asks, "Do you believe in God?"

"Yes. I do believe in God."

"God works in many ways. If you assume the persona of the Messiah to teach your philosophy of love what harm is done?"

"But isn't that a lie?"

"You may miss a once in a lifetime opportunity. Getting your trust in God message heard is more important than scrupling over a public image that may or may not be truthful. God promised a Messiah. You may in fact be the Messiah. You don't know everything. Would you think that God would tell his son everything? God works in wondrous ways. Who are you to judge? He didn't say the Messiah would look or sound like a Moses encore. Isn't the mere fact that a Messiah was promised indicate that God wanted to take all people to the next level via a new path and a new leader? You may be the Messiah. That's good enough for me." Peter almost recites this argument. It was rehearsed and laid in wait for its time. Peter is clever and has an innate sense of timing.

Jesus answers, "OK Peter. Do your Messiah thing. But I will never say that I am the Messiah. If some one asks me that question. I will deny that I'm the Messiah.

So be warned. You had better 'tweak' your marketing pitch accordingly. And I've a question for you Peter. Do you believe in God? Or is this whole scheme just about money and power?"

Peter turned and left. Jesus was sure Peter had heard the question but choose not to answer. So the bargain was made between Jesus and the producers.

"What do you think John? Did I make a bad bargain?"

"I certainly don't trust him. But the burden is really on him to deliver his promises. If he can't deliver your new make over or if he fails to set up desirable venues and adequate advertising then you drop out."

"That's true. But for me to allow this hustler to market me as the Messiah crosses a lot of lines in the sand. Now I can't claim ignorance. Because I know now what the plan is. But who will I have offended? If people are drawn to me because of the Messiah advertising and after they hear my genuine honest advice and they profit themselves by taking that advice, isn't it worth the small deception?"

John answers with a degree of insight that surprises Jesus," There is no such thing as a small deception. There are only small bad consequences because of small deceptions. That's if you are lucky. Do you feel lucky Jesus? Small deceptions can lead to horrible unintended consequences of Homeric proportions if things break the wrong way."

Jesus is shaken. It's as if John just gave him a glimpse of what was to come. And for the first time in Jesus' life, he was worried. Jesus thought, welcome to the life of an adult. My words and actions have consequences. I can't blame others now. I am it. He looked back at the monks. No wonder they were so serene. They lived a child's life. No worries because they relied on higher ups to run the monasteries and organize the delivering of alms. But now Jesus with one quick nod of his head catapulted himself from a drone to the leader of a new branch or interpretation of an old religion. The new branch was his introduction of Buddhism to the west. But to accomplish that feat he could be rightfully accused of trashing the laws of Moses and Abraham and the teachings of the scriptures regarding the Messiah. It was like John's evaluation. There are no small deceptions. How would he navigate through the seas of settled religion and political pressure to come though the other side and deliver harmony on earth. Many before him had tried and failed and caused great grief to themselves and to their followers. How was he going to make the earth a better place by making it a more complicated place? His tutor once said, "Keep it simple stupid". Now he finally knew what he had meant.

"Well it's settled John. I won't go back. I'm tired of Jerusalem. I'm fed up with the status quo. I would rather go up in flames trying something big than just wasting away and end up like Peter. Maybe he's right. Maybe I'm the Messiah. What are the worth of words without actions? I promise good actions and if the words don't actually match who I am, so be it. Your actions speak volumes of the joys of not taking life too seriously. Hanging out in the river is your way of expressing that creed. Well my way is more danger-ous but it will compensate by experiencing joy from challenging boredom head on. Boredom is the curse of the human. Animals live in the moment and don't fret about what might have been. So here I go."

"Don't knock animals 'living in the moment'. You just described my life style. Think about, that's all you really have, that's all I have that's mine. It's the only space that I control — the moment. The Romans say *nunc ipsum* — there is only the moment. So make the most of it. Because Peter and his producer friend John will probably write your history for their benefit. It's an old story. You are the visionary and Peter and John are the bean counters that convert your teachings and life's examples into money. They will found a religion based on you. I'll bet you wouldn't recognize yourself if some how you were able to read your life's story a hundred years from now. I am going back to my bend in the river. That's my refuge and kingdom. I will be at the gathering. Let me know time and place."

John leaves. Jesus is unsettled. But the plans are made and it's all forward now.

Chapter IV
Jesus and the Producers

For the next month, Peter and partner John used every resource at their disposal to give Jesus a new look and a new wardrobe. It was a look and wardrobe that was designed to attest to his credibility before Jesus even opened his mouth. John's wife had a friend who worked in Pontius Pilate's household. Her name was Ruth. She would salvage things from the governors household. In return Ruth would get fish with salt and without sand. This turned into a cascade of stuff including razors and scissors for that close shave and haircut. Ruth saw enough haircuts at the governors compound to advise on how to cut and shape Jesus' hair. She delivered many near-new sandals imported from Italy. Also light weight robes that were fitted by John's wife to Jesus' specifications. A marvelous

Tyrian Purple cloak was delivered. It was a singular color in which a little red was apparent. It was reserved for members of the Roman imperial court. The color was derived from a mollusk that was found offshore Phoenicia. In their greed, no thought was given to the suspicions that would be aroused when Jesus, a man of the people showed up with this purple cape draped from his broad shoulders. Fingernails had to be manicured. Pilates own nippers were "rescued" after falling on the floor. Portions of bath oils and colognes from Egypt were poured into pocket size containers. Also emollients of the kind that accompanied the pharaoh Ramses II travel bag when he was interred in the Valley of the Kings were delivered in the original gold leaf wrapping. All was smuggled out by the sneaky Ruth.

Peter and John made inquires about venues to feature the gatherings. The amphitheater idea was quickly discarded. It was too expensive. It was decided that an open air setting in the late afternoon a short distance from town would make do. They didn't know how many people would show up. So the large natural amphitheater aspects of the vacant land would surely serve well. Peter, John and John the Baptist would all pitch in. They would offer fish at cost. But attendees would be encouraged to offer something for admittance. It was thought the first gathering would be near free as to develop a market. Free samples were a proven marketing gambit.

Now came time for Peter and John to contact Jesus and review what Jesus would say and how long it would take. John the Baptist also came. They all met at the planned gathering site.

Peter asked, "Jesus, what have you decided to talk about?"

Jesus answered in a subtly different voice. It was more humble yet there was an undertone that demanded what he said was to be taken seriously. It was apparent that Jesus had morphed. Could he now believed that he was the Messiah?

"It's all here. Let me read you some passages. *Blessed are the poor in spirit, for theirs is the kingdom of heaven. Blessed are the meek, for they should inherit the earth. Blessed are they who mourn for they shall be comforted. Blessed are they who hunger and thirst for they shall be satisfied. Blessed are the merciful, for they shall obtain mercy. Blessed are the clean of heart for they shall see God* . . . and it goes on. And the first part ends with. *Rejoice and exult because your reward is great in heaven.*"

Peter answers, "That's perfect."

John nods approvingly. John the Baptist is pleased. But the Baptist would be impressed and pleased if someone sensibly spoke more than three words in succession.

Peter continues, "Jesus, is the rest of the text like these?"

"Yes. I estimate that my address will take about 45 minutes to an hour. It could run longer if there are many questions."

Peter answers, "I can help you with the crowd. I can manage the amount and length of the questions. We don't want them interrupting or cutting your full message short. Would you consider adding something to your prepared notes?"

"What did you have in mind?"

"In your own words, and that is key for credibility could you obliquely refer to the obligations of the wealthy and powerful in Jerusalem to also help with Gods work?"

"These are my teachings. You think them banal because you never heard them before. You think like most men. If it isn't advice on how someone will make money then why bother to listen. You don't fool me. I made a bargain with you and John so I could get my message out. I know you see a pay day with me. But make no mistake. This is the message. And It will be spoken by me. That's the way it's going to be. Are you in or do you want to go back to the fishing business?"

The irony of the "are you in?" phrase wasn't lost on Peter and John. John looked at Peter and nodded acceptance of Jesus' terms.

"We are in."

John asked," Would you object to an opening act before your sermon?

"What kind of opening act?"

"It will be in good taste and entertain and relax the crowd. The more relaxed the group the more your talk will sink in. It will enhance the whole experience. I will personally write up the act using themes that you will speak about. Please give me a copy of the sermon so I may have a guide."

Jesus replies, "OK. But I'll remember your promise. I don't want my presentation cheapened."

John continues, "By the way, I ran into that merchant from India you talked about. He asked me if you're still interested in some soma? He has some."

"No. I'm finished with soma."

Chapter V
The Sermon on the Mount and the Torch Singer

t was early evening. It was a beautiful night for an out door event. People had been arriving in singles, doubles and small groups for the past hour. Advertising and word of mouth paid off. There were at least a couple hundred already. And the event wasn't scheduled to start for another hour. They were spread out according to relationships. They mostly all came from Jerusalem. Many had brought their own food, drink and blankets. Peter and John were making some sales of fish. But the producers paid less and less attention to fish mongering. They were increasingly excited and moved by the people who were coming. The attendees were serious. John and Peter were touched. It's like they had discovered a valuable natural resource. But this wasn't gold or silver. These were people in need.

They had the potential to be infinitely more valuable than gold. They were looking for help and guidance. Under the right circumstances could lift the producers onto a world stage along with Jesus. Even the coldly calculating Peter melted some what when he thought of the burden that the people were putting on his management group and Jesus to deliver. Their posters and word of mouth had made contact with a vast unmet need. If this evenings turnout was at all representative of the worlds peoples then indeed there was a huge market of people that were seeking guidance and fulfillment. They almost felt ashamed of their mercantile ploys to get these people here under the lure of their created Messiah. They were humbled. They now made extra effort to make the attendees welcome. They even gave free fish to people who were without food.

Particularly John was moved by the peoples perceived need. John had shaved his beard and cut his hair short. He had flowers in his hair. He replaced his traditional full length robe with a short sleeved shirt and a v-shaped neckline. This went with shorts. Also there were baubles, bangles and beads around his neck. John had morphed. John's demeanor had also changed somewhat. He was more mellow. He had been working with the gal in the opening act for the past two weeks.

The young woman came from Egypt. John's relative there put Nefrateri in touch with the producer John. Peter had not met her. He only knew that she could sing some and supposedly had world class looks. That was fine with him.

John said in a genuinely tearful way, "These people ache. They hurt. I hope we can give them something tonight that they can take away that will give them comfort."

Earlier Peter had noticed the flowers in John's hair, the clean shave and short hair and the hip clothing, but he didn't remark. Although John's absence for two weeks did make him wonder. But now, it was unmistakeable some event or events had changed John forever. The flowers etc., the absence alone with the singer, the new mellowness combined with the tearful remarks about the people made Peter think of a soma experience. Soma changed Jesus. Did it change John? Had John got into the soma? Or was the theatrical wardrobe a ploy? It would compliment the look and feel of Jesus and his message? Maybe John was test marketing a new line of clothing and accoutrement? Peter would look for signs of imitation by others in town in the next few days. If people started wearing their hair short and shaving their beards he would come out with a new line of clothing and make a killing. No matter what John was up to, Peter was in it for the money.

The advertising presented Jesus as the Messiah. There was no hedging about it. The producers were shooting dice. The downside would be that they lost Jesus because of blasphemy charges. But they would still have the basis of a religion. The posters effectively offered free access to the "promised one". Jesus would talk about his trust in God philosophy. He would also talk about the world to come and how people could almost mimic that promised world now on this earth and in their own time. Prepare and live it now was a catchy way to attract people. And later Jesus would take questions.

The posters also mentioned preliminary entertainment. She was a "torch singer" from Egypt. It was claimed that she was descendant from Egyptian royalty and was a "stunning beauty". Her name was Nefrateri. She would dramatize and sing an original composition for this evenings sermon. John had collaborated with the singer for two weeks. They composed a song and choreographed a simple presentation. There were no musicians. She was more about beauty and dramatic acting than about singing. She was more torch than singer. And the singing was more singsongy. But with her body swaying in heavenly garments, who wouldn't feel satisfied? Nefrateri was indeed beautiful. She was in her late twenties, but she had a look on her face that showed she had been through a lot of disappointments. Yet she still had a pluckiness and wonderful smile. The shadow of some disappointment in her lovely face gave her character. It made her more appealing. She now was more of a love interest for a broader spectrum of people. She carried herself with self esteem and pride. She must have been a target of lust from early in her life. It seems she took away more bad memories than good from those experiences. But somehow she prevailed and paradoxically was better for it. A cosmopolitan, beautiful and poised woman is indeed an attraction.

John had worked on getting her outfitted appropriately. He requested women clothing from Ruth. He also gave some of the precious emollients and oils to Nefrateri. She instinctively knew what to do with them. There was eye shadow and rouge for the cheeks and her luscious lips. They also used a light sprinkle of gold-like specs for her hair. They both decided that she would wear a magnificent diaphanous gown. Nefrateri was tall. The dress belonged to Pilate's lover. But she had a closet full. It wouldn't be missed. It would be a show stopping sight to behold, as it would be modified in a provocative way. The neckline would plunge to the waist, while the upper area material would be cropped up and supportive of her beautiful breasts. The right side of the dress would be split along a centered leg vector. The outfit together with a choreographed arm and leg movements would alternately accentuate the breasts and then the leg. She would be a swaying metronome of exotic and erotic appeal. There were also heavenly sandals. Her hair would be up. It would compliment her beautiful long neck. In another time, Nefrateri could have been a pharaoh's wife. But now is not then. So she's the torch singer for the producers.

It was getting near show time. The venue was getting crowded. At least a thousand people were already seated and more were coming. The people were well behaved. It looked as if many had somewhat dressed up for the occasion. They took it seriously. John looked for Peter and Jesus. John wanted to start shortly. He had planned to add a measure of drama with the setting sun and how it illuminated Nefrateri and Jesus while they were in front of the audience. Also he didn't want to end the gathering prematurely because of darkness. Peter and John noticed some stand offish observers. They weren't part of the greater group. Jesus and his producers were attracting scrutiny. This was about turf. It was about power. It was about money. Who cared that much? It had to be the powers that be. The powers were either the Romans or the downtown rabbis. Maybe both were represented at opening night.

John climbs a small hillock in front of the crowd. He is outlined against the horizon. The crowd is facing east. So the sun is slowing setting behind them in the west. There is a gentle prevailing westerly wind. The wind sweeps into the crowd. He holds up his arms to get the peoples attention. He speaks.

"Good evening ladies and gentlemen. Welcome to our new world. Jesus will be speaking later. I know that you are all eager to hear what the promised one has to say. He will not disappoint. I promise you that. All we in management ask is that if you like what you hear tonight please tell a friend and both of you please return to our next scheduled event. So without further ado, I would like to present this evenings featured entertainment. Her name is Nefrateri. That's all I need say because everything else she has and does speaks for itself. Nefrateri ladies and gentlemen, lets give her some encouragement." John claps and the crowd follows his lead. Nefrateri walks on to the stage as if she's been doing it for her whole life. The crowd notices her enchanting looks and demeanor and they quicken their applause. They also notice her diaphanous gown. The sun shines through its gossamer weave to reveal a voluptuous body. She has no under garments. The full figure includes inviting thighs that feature the jet nest and magnificent breasts. It will only get more intriguing as the angle of the suns rays sinks lower. Some men whistle and some stand up. That draws swift looks of condemnation from their accompanying dates. But the point is made and remembered by the women that the bar has been raised and there's no going back. Nefrateri soaks in the admiration as if she were soaking in a bath of priceless Egyptian scented oils. Speaking of which, the scents slowly waft out over the crowd. That's why these scents are so expensive and valuable. They last longer and cover a larger distance and they have a divine aroma. They speak volumes to the simple. It's a language that is understood. She waits till the crowd finishes and grows quiet. Everyone is still. It's a rare moment. John is a few feet away. Sitting on the ground his eyes are filled with love for Nefrateri and joy for his new life.

Nefrateri recites her song in a speaking-on-pitch style. It's almost like a soliloquy. Which makes the crowd feel they are peeping in Nefrateri's boudoir. There are only different calibrations of high and low intonations depending on the dramatic import of the words. Added to the words are expressive body movements that show to advantage her natural beauty. The choreography of Nefrateri's presentation is neatly hidden to look like improvisation. She's has natural rhythm.

"Thank you for your warm greeting. I will tell you of my experiences and what I learned. These lessons have sustained me through many challenges. Some have been exalting triumphs and some have not been.

But I take what comes and do not complain. I want to thank everyone I've ever met. The good and the bad have made me what I am today. I regret nothing. To have not met any one would have indeed been a regret.

I have met Jesus. He talked to me of many things. And its as if I knew him from another time and another place. We looked more than we spoke. Yet I felt informed. The truth of yesterday is still the truth of today.

Only the names of things, places and people change. Names are sometimes meant to deceive. So look and see what is beneath the name. There is the truth. The good and the bad are always with us.

In fact we couldn't have good unless we had bad. Otherwise how could one tell the difference? Trust in God. He doesn't deceive. For he doesn't put names on things. We do that. So if there is bad and if there is good, it is we that cause it.

Avoid tools. For if you use a tool you lose your place. The greatest of all tools is talk. The more you talk and listen the greater chance for confusion. For words have different meanings for different persons. Look at actions. They speak truth.

The second greatest tool is money. It is an alchemy to invite deception and laziness. Too many things can be influenced by money and yet it is a hollow exercise. Sweat will buy more than money. And a feeling of well-deserved replaces a nagging hunger.

Take responsibility for your life. Never feel at a loss. Because change is in your hands. Therefore you can mock the passing of time along as long as you are engaged happily. There is no time if there is no change.

All during her talk, she swayed and moved across the stage area. Sometimes she would gracefully kneel and then recline. All the while letting the flowing gown slip slowly to expose her naked body. Then she would continue to speak but accentuate with a thrusting leg or a head thrown back. They were simple moves. But natural grace and timing can enhance any gesture. Her body riveted the attention of the crowd. But early on her words took over and the people were moved by their substance, until she was one experience of beauty and wisdom. The audience was in a rapture. A tearful John was pleased with his script. Peter felt Nefrateri had nailed the message of Jesus by underscoring the words with her fabulous physical presentation. John the Baptist face waxed philosophical. That was probably the greatest compliment that went unnoticed. Even Jesus looked vulnerable and in her power. The suspicious observers had much earlier stop taking notes and just watched peacefully. Such is the power of simple words and simple graceful movements and classical beauty. Poetry in motion is what the sculptures and painters seek to capture. Nefrateri finished and barely bowed from the waist. The crowd was spellbound. Only after a pause was there a slight applause as if to not break the rapture. John walked on stage. He said a few quiet words as he took her hands. He gave her a loving embrace. They kissed. It was apparent that the rough cut Jew and the Egyptian beauty were an item. Then he escorted her to a private area out of view.

And now it was time for Jesus. But before that John

addressed the group about something that was not on the original evenings scheduled events. He carried a sheaf of papers. He faced the crowd and waited for them to give him their attention. He spoke in a energetic enthusiastic voice.

"Dear friends. Before Jesus comes out. I have a few words of my own that I would like to say. Simply Jesus has changed my life. Before meeting him, I was a struggling fisherman. My personal life was without excitement. My marriage was without love. And my prospects were for more of the same. But things have changed because of the Messiahs influence. I'm now part of his flock. And I hope you all will consider yourselves a part also. My wife and I are now divorced. I have a new love and together with her we will explore new adventures. Also my mind has been permanently expanded with a new cosmic consciousness. I owe this transformation to an herb that Jesus described. It's called soma. Tides and the size of my fish catch are no longer in the front of my mind. This plant has opened to me a heavenly vista. I would like to share a portion of what I experienced. It's my Book of Revelations. Here in part are some of my recollections from the mind trip that I took after taking soma."

John began, *"I looked and beheld a door standing*

open in heaven and a voice said, 'Come up hither and I will show thee things that must come to pass hereafter.' Immediately I was made a spirit and beheld a throne set in heaven. And upon this throne he was sitting. And I saw a new heaven and a new earth. For the first heaven and the first earth passed away and the sea and the fish are no more. And I saw the holy city, New Jerusalem coming down out of heaven from God. Made ready as a bride for her husband. And he on the throne said, 'Behold the dwelling of God with men and he will dwell with men. And they will be his people. And God will wipe away every tear from their eyes. And death will be no more nor mourning. Nor crying nor pain any more for the former things have passed away.'"

John finished. He had wound himself tight with the telling of his soma aided experience. The people did not know what to make of it. They only were sure that it authentic.

John continued, "With the help of Jesus and soma and my beloved, I have peeled off the handed down traditions of over a thousand years of peer pressure. The condemning finger pointing at me of my shortcomings is gone. I banished it. I have my own value now. The pressure to accumulate is gone. Those were the implied laws of Abraham and Moses. But they are now gone from my mind. I am now happy to be a nobody. I was a nobody before. But now I am not ashamed to be a nobody. I urge all to be a nobody. For in oblivion do we expand ourselves and feel comfortable no matter where we venture. Before I thought that only money and power made some one important. And now I enjoy each day whether I have money or power or not. Poverty can be lived and enjoyed.

So now as I promised here's the promised Jesus. Jesus walks up to the hillock from the side. It's a lovely evening and the sun features him on the personal horizon of the gathering. He is striking in his appearance. His cropped light hair is still long enough to lay down. He shaved just hours before. The emollients have deep cleaned his fair skin. His fine features belie any trace of semitic blood. The Tyrian robe drapes his tunic and both stop just above the knees. The light hair gives the impression that he's without bodily hair. The golden sandals and the pungent fragrant cologne complete the picture of what could be a patrician of the imperial court. In a completely natural gesture he opens his arms wide as to welcome all.

He speaks, "Thank you all for coming. I have come to this place for one purpose. I want to comfort all of you. So many of us feel inadequate to the challenges of life. Many after a short time give up. They say to themselves, 'I can't keep up', or 'the world has already picked the winners and the losers and I am too late to challenge the rich and powerful'. I am here to say, 'Forget those thoughts'. You, each of you, are special to God and to me. You have a place in nature. Indeed you are part of nature and nature has all you will ever need. You only have to do one thing to survive and be content. And that is to put away the greed of man's culture. Adjust your attitude and appetites so that you and others may easily achieve what is provided by our heavenly father through his wonderful and myriad creation of the natural world. Only use what is needed. Leave some for the rest that are to follow. *Too many people lay up for themselves treasures on earth where rust and moths consume and where thieves break in and steal. But instead lay up for yourselves treasures in heaven where neither rust nor moths will consume nor where thieves break in and steal. For where thy treasure is so be the place of your heart. No man can serve two masters for he will either hate the one or love the other or stand by one and despise the other. You cannot serve two masters. You cannot serve God and also money. Therefore do not be anxious saying what shall we eat or what shall we drink? Or what are we to put* on? For your father in heaven knows you need all these things. But first seek the kingdom of God and his justice and all these things shall be given to you besides. Do not be anxious for tomorrow for tomorrow will have its own anxieties. Sufficient for you to worry about today and face tomorrow when it comes."

Jesus paused. "Are there any questions?"

A man in the front part of the audience asks, "How will my master respond if I slow my work speed to feel more comfortable. Shall I say that God is my true master and my salary is not as important as my peace of mind?"

"Give to your earthly master what is due him. But reserve your loyalty to your God in heaven."

"My clothes have holes. How can trust in God close those holes?"

"Do not sweat the small stuff." Jesus responds.

Some of the crowd are confused by the flip answers of Jesus. Others don't even think his answers through but rather marvel at his looks and clothes and the confidence of his voice.

Jesus continues, "Everyone therefore who hears these my words and acts upon them shall be likened to wise man who built his house on rock, And the rain fell and the floods came and the winds blew and beat against the house but it did not fall because it was founded on rock. And everyone who hears my words and does not act upon them shall be likened to a foolish man who built his house on sand. And the rain fell and the floods came and the winds blew and beat against the house and it fell and was utterly ruined."

Some one in the crowd asked, "You speak in parables Jesus. I do not have a house. I would take one on sand or rock. What do you say to me?"

"As I said earlier. *God will provide. Make do while on earth but lay up wealth in Gods kingdom.*"

The same person followed up with another question. It was as if he was trying to tangle Jesus. Jesus thought the face of the questioner looked somewhat familiar. Where had he seen this man before? He got the feeling that this man meant harm.

He asked," How will we get along in this world without a house, without clothes and without food if God doesn't help? Because I have noticed many people who have not been provided for."

"I didn't say it would be easy. But if you notice people who are hungry and without homes and without enough clothing you should try to help. God will bless you."

The man persisted with yet another question."

Should the Romans help with alms giving."

That question did it. Now Jesus remembered where he had seen the questioner before. It was about a week ago when Jesus and John the Baptist ran into Peter in Jerusalem. Jesus saw Peter walking with this man just before Peter spotted the Baptist and himself. Peter noticed Jesus and waved off the questioner-companion to go away. So Peter through this plant in the crowd is trying to get Jesus to endorse social welfare. That would clearly take Jesus across a line into challenging settled Roman occupying law. Depending how he answered he could be calling for his own death warrant. But he had to say something or lose credibility with the audience. And so Jesus answered,

"Any one who notices these shortfalls in their societies should help. It is an obligation from one man to another to do charitable work. But do the help quietly so only the person who receives and God know of your good deeds. Do not try to profit from gossip of good deeds. The Romans are free to do what they please." Jesus thought he answered cleverly. Maybe he would survive to carry on his work. But he found out that Peter was no friend. He was in it for himself. He didn't care about anyone else. Peter didn't care if Jesus lived or died. Maybe Peter actually preferred a dead martyr. It could be better for business. The religion business brings out the best and the worse in people.

A questioner from the rear asks, "Do you speak for God?"

"I speak for myself. My advice is simple. *Do unto others what you would have them do to you. Ask and it shall be given you, seek and you shall find. Knock and it shall be opened to you. For everyone who asks receives and he who seeks finds and to whom that knocks it shall be opened. What man among you who if his son asks him for a loaf will hand him a stone or if he asks for a fish will hand him a serpent? Therefore if you as inadequate as you are know how to give good gifts to your children how much more will your father in heaven give good things to those that ask him?*"

The same questioner says, "Are you the Messiah?"

Jesus answered, "Do I have to be the Messiah for my words to be believed and revered? What have you heard here tonight that you take exception?"

"I don't want the force of government and their laws to force me to provide for strangers. Charity is a personal matter. Work is a personal matter. Who has the power tell me that my work is for some one else's benefit?"

Jesus answered, "Do you pay taxes?"

"Yes. We all pay taxes."

"You already provide your labor for another persons project. All I say is that you help people who truly need. Rome has its agenda you should have your own. But personal charity to the needy is more worthy."

The questioner persisted, "The advertising posters claim you to be the Messiah. Are you the Messiah?"

"The poster says I am the Messiah. I do not say I am the Messiah."

"Jesus you can't have it both ways. Tell us finally. Are you the Messiah?"

"I am who you thank I am? I can't change your thoughts. Only you can choose to change your opinions." Jesus scanned the audience looking for Peter. He had questions for him when he left the stage.

The questioner ceased. It would seem that what he came for he got. And what he got was something that he could use against Jesus. The exchange between Christ and the sharp interrogator produced nuanced responses that could be twisted in a court hearing to bring a judgment of inciting rebellion. For example, Jesus didn't deny that he was the Messiah? That omission could imply that he thought he was. If that were true then Jesus would have to face the Sanhedrin for blasphemy. That group was the final arbiter. Also,

Christ preached to the people that they ask for help from those could help. Did that mean Rome was responsible to use tax money to subsidize the poor in Jerusalem? That would be a first. Pilate would hear about that answer. Also there was the judgment by Jesus that personal charity was more worthy than paying taxes to Rome. One of these responses by itself could invite a follow up investigation by Rome or the Sanhedrin. But all three responses at the same time and at the same place in front of hundreds of witnesses was certain to bring charges. Particularly the preaching of Gods agenda being more important than Rome's agenda was the most troubling for Jesus. Rome or the Sanhedrin could swoop in. Or maybe the Sanhedrin would be the one to respond more viciously, since all politics are local? And if Jesus finally reveals himself as the son of God then the local rabbis of the Sanhedrin would be out of business or severely compromised.

The crowd had no more questions. They were a little put off by the testy exchange between Jesus and the interrogator. It broke the mood.

John got up on the stage and spoke, "Thank you all for coming tonight. Please come again. We will notify you about the time and date of our next gathering."

The people clapped warmly and left at leisurely

pace. They talked amongst themselves about Nefrateri and Jesus. They buzzed about this less work and more benefits as a birth right. This was a very appealing prospect. It should have been thought up long before this. Maybe they could get retro compensation for the over sight? Religion now made more sense to them. There was a real reason to believe in the hereafter.

Jesus was followed by many who wanted to speak with him privately. He still took furtive glances about to locate Peter. But Peter was occupied with another who wanted to speak to him. The person who pressed Jesus about his Messiah claim caught up with Peter in the back of the audience.

"Peter, can I have a word with you please?"

Peter said, "Certainly. What did you think of the show tonight?"

"I wasn't disappointed," he said cryptically. "What is your relationship with Jesus?"

"You have the advantage of me sir. You know who I am but I do not who you are. What is your name and why did you ask me about my relationship with Jesus?"

"My name is Saul. I'm from Tarsus. I am the scribe for the Sanhedrin. I was sent here tonight by them to collect information about the claim of Messiah by your Jesus."

Peter tenses up and becomes very judicial, "What specifically do you want to ask?"

"Whose idea was the claim of Messiah?"

"Jesus claims to be the Messiah. That was his idea."

"What is your relationship with Jesus?"

"I and my partner John, he was the master of ceremonies, are employed by Jesus to manage his public appearances."

"Do you believe Jesus is the Messiah?"

"I do not believe in God. I have skills as an impresario and I limit myself to those skills."

"Did you or John write any of the material that Jesus' uses?"

"No. He insists on writing his own stuff."

"Are you familiar with the law regarding blasphemy?"

"No. I am apolitical and I am not religious. I did not break any law that I knew existed."

"Ignorance of the law is no excuse. The Sanhedrin is watchful for people who break the laws regarding blasphemy. Where do you live?"

"My partner John and I fish in the Sea of Galilee. We are there most of the time."

"We will be in touch with you if we need further information. Thank you and good night"

Peter was very nervous and shocked how fast the Sanhedrin was protecting its religious turf. He was now caught between Jesus who he betrayed to the scribe and the Sanhedrin who wanted him for abetting Jesus' blasphemy. Jesus would be dead within weeks. No doubt about that. Peter felt some sorrow for Jesus. He wasn't a bad person. His only faults were naivete and being spoiled by his mother. The Sanhedrin are the bad guys. The fact is who holds the power decides who or what is bad and who or what is good. What a brutal life we live in.

It's like Nefrateri said, "Trust in God. He doesn't deceive. For he doesn't put names on things. We do that. So if there is bad and if there is good, it is we that cause it." She was right about that. Except there is no God and only trust your skills to see you through. In hindsight the only guy who had it right was John the Baptist. He had his bend in the river. Women showed up voluntarily to get bathed and have a fling. And then they left. No ties. No guilt. Ah. That's the way to go. The baptist wouldn't lose his head with those kind of relationships.

Peter had to get out of town. His one chance at the big time had turned into a possible death sentence within a months time. His head is swimming.

He thinks the game is rigged. I am a rookie compared to these professionals. But on second thought, all his work is not a loss. He has discovered valuable knowledge about what will motivate people. The great value of his knowledge is validated by the Sanhedrin response. If it wasn't a powerful knowledge then the Sanhedrin wouldn't bother. So this is life at the top? These are the risks and rewards of the major players in world religions and politics.

He is no longer a humble fisherman. He's going ahead. He will be the founder of a new religion. It will be a catholic universal religion. He won't have Jesus. But Jesus won't be around much longer anyway. Jesus will be history soon. But Peter will have a bona fide martyr as the founder of his church. That's a jackpot legacy. And I am the legitimate successor to Jesus. Actually he is somewhat my creation. I have copies of his speeches. I have some of his garments. I have a copy of John's Revelations that is a direct result of the teachings of Jesus. Soma, mustn't forget soma. That could be a side source of income. I can write some of my accounts of my conversations with Jesus. He won't be around to dispute them.

Miracles? There will be lots of miracles. Whose to stop me? He actually used me to promote his philosophy. I can tell that story. I've heard of Simon Magus in Rome. He routinely sells access to the heaven and also offers positions in his synagogue for money or barter. I can do that. My Messiah Jesus trumps his stale Mosaic views. Simon Magus is a niche player. He's under the targets of Roman spears. They don't consider him a threat because he addresses only religious people.

My target is the religious and political individual. Rome won't like that. So I have to move fast in Rome. Make a quick hit and then hit the road. Maybe I will retire to a Greek island? The Roman infrastructure will be the body of my universal church. I'm going to need some help with organization. John ran off with the torch singer. I'm going to start from scratch. John's plan and this evenings real market launch was more successful than expectations. The Sanhedrin immediate response proved that. So next up is Rome. Rome is the place to launch the church. The city is so large that they will not notice me. And when my followers have grown large in number, the Emperor would not dare challenge them. Maybe I'll offer Caesar a deal? How about a proconsul position for me in exchange for partial control over my flock? So Peter, are you up to the challenge? You had better get your message of Jesus to Rome before the Sanhedrin and Pilate catch up to you." Peter has a bounce in his step. He will go home and pack. Next stop Rome. There are trading ships leaving from Tyre in Phoenicia on a weekly schedule. He will try to catch one. He would never see Jesus again.

The scribe reported back to the Sanhedrin. A clever response by the Sanhedrin was put into motion that was necessitated by Roman occupying laws. Only the Romans could carry out death penalties. The locals still had the power of indictment and trial but the execution was mandated to the Romans. So the Sanhedrin would drag Jesus before Pilate and demand that Rome carry out the ruling of the rabbis.

Chapter VI
Jesus Cures Possessed Boy

t was a few days after the sermon and Jesus was enjoying an early morning walk on the outskirts of Jerusalem. He had noticed that in town more and more young men wore their hair short and were clean shaven. Some of those had cropped their robes to knee length. He obviously had made contact. He thought, where would it all end? Could he be as successful as the monks in India? Could he replace personal greed with social consciousness and charity? The beautiful day made it hard for him to focus on the affairs of man. Those matters resembled a sea that was constantly raging. The fresh air and the warm rays of the sun and the chirping of the birds provided a simple and deeply pleasurable experience. So he gave into natures influence and blotted his mind of religion, politics and

what the future held. But it didn't last long. His fame now started to make demands on him. A voice called his name. It seemed a distant voice. His reverie was shattered. He turned his head. It was a woman who was actually close by.

She said, "Are you Jesus?"

"Yes. I am he."

"We caught your show the other night. My husband and I really were inspired. Your words gave us hope that we could somehow make it in this world with help from friends and neighbors. We all have to look out for each other," said the cute young woman. She was simply dressed, but she wore her hair up.

"Thank you for your kind words." Jesus noticed her western styled hair. Didn't the torch singer also have her hair up in the first act? But he wanted to get back to his day dreaming and so he resumed his walk.

"Please Jesus. If you have a moment. We have a fifteen year old son who is a problem for us. He joined us at the talk the other night. But he was bored by your words and fidgeted. He said, 'Jesus doesn't talk my language because he doesn't think like me or Archimedes and Democritus'. The boy is withdrawn and consumed with two books which are filled with strange figures and even stranger conclusions. The words are in another language. The notations and diagrams are troublesome. One figure in particular is evil. It is the Mogen David. But our boy calls it a hexagram. My husband and I are afraid he is possessed by the devil. You are a holy man. Could you meet with him and rid him of his devil?"

Jesus thought to himself, so much for the walk. "Surely I'll meet him. What is his name?"

"His name is Isaac. He's at home now. It's only a short distance from here."

Jesus and the woman arrive and enter the modest house. It is in the middle of a small piece of land that includes a garden and farm animals. There is also fish being cured in a smoker. The woman and her husband are subsistence farmers. The young boy is inside the house. He is at a table next to the only window that now has sun light shining through. Isaac is reading the book. He's looking at the figures in the book and sometimes he copies the figures onto paper. He copies the figures so as to follow the logic that the author of the book says exists in those figures.

The woman's name is Anne. She speaks, "Isaac. I have brought Jesus to meet you. Do you remember him from the other night ? We all went to his show. Please put aside your book and shake his hand."

Isaac reminds Jesus of himself just a few minutes ago. James was lost in his own reverie of contemplation and resented being dragged back into the mundane. The dark haired boy dutifully rises from the table and extends his small hand. He's a little short for his age. His clothes are clean. He is very well mannered. His face and eyes reflect an inner intensity. They are shaped by the rigors of relentless mental speculation.

Jesus speaks first as is the custom that the older commences the conversation, "Please to meet you Isaac."

The boy deferentially nods his head. He awaits further cues. He wants this meeting over as soon as possible. He wont make it easy.

Jesus asks, "I am sorry Isaac to disturb you. What are you reading?"

"Right now, it's a book by Archimedes. It's a fascinating collection of diagrams, theories and equations. The diagrams are analytically described by Archimedes. He deals with basic truths. No matter what the size or place. No matter what the composition —animal, vegetable or mineral — the rules still apply. His observations give me comfort. They make me feel at home on this earth. I know now there is a reason for everything. This may interest you. I arrive at the same comfort level that you teach. But I arrive through scientific and mathematical proofs. You say, 'Don't worry God will provide'. Archimedes actually instructs one how to let nature, or if you prefer God, do that providing. And if nature or God are busy elsewhere Archimedes gives you a do-it-yourself book of instructions. It certainly beats praying or sleeping. I also have a book by Democritus. He is also a Greek and a mathematician. In addition he is a philosopher. When one speculates about atoms it becomes necessarily a philosophical exercise, because its difficult to prove their existence. One has to have faith. "

Jesus asks, "Do you have faith? Do you believe in God?"

"I am aware of a master plan in the planetary movements. Both Democritus and Archimedes led me to this conclusion. And I further surmise that the same mathematical principles of nature in the heavens are the same that influence our earth. But to answer your question directly. I still am not sure there is a master that goes with this master plan."

Jesus asks, "What is your reason for not embracing a God who created all that we see?"

"It's paradoxical. Although there is a regularity to heavenly movements that are mimicked here on earth there is also the stark truth that everything is constantly changing or morphing into another form. Now I ask you 'Why would a God create constant change?"

Jesus is stuck for an immediate explanation, "Perhaps God wants to test us?"

"Why should we mere mortals be tested? After all if God created us he certainly must know are performance specifications. Aren't you supposed to be the son of God?"

Anne jumps in when she hears a certain arrogance to Isaac's question, "Isaac. You must show respect to all. This certainly includes our guest the good Jesus. He's trying to help you."

"Sorry mother. I meant no disrespect to Jesus. But I only asked that question in that tone because it's the same tone I use myself to myself when I am conducting a thought experiment. I apologize Jesus if I offended you. Mother, you demonstrate the downside effects of collectivism. Merely asking questions isn't arrogant, although our religious and secular leaders would make us believe so. They don't want questions about their policies because that would threaten their rule. We have a poor culture. We are like dung beetles. Consequently we pick on ourselves because we have no lush gardens to pick from. Mother you could have been a legendary heroic Amazon if you wore born 1000 mile east of here. But you weren't and so we all are here and we are what we are. "

Jesus asks, "What is the essence of your observations?"

"I can't take sole credit for what I think because Archimedes and Democritus pointed the way but I speculate that the central controlling force is centripetal. It causes all moving bodies to move in a curve or elliptical course. I suspect the sun is the source of that centripetal force. Some mistake it for God. Maybe I will change my mind later in life about the existence of God."

"Where did you get these books?

Isaac loosens up his interrogatory attitude towards Jesus and his intrusion. Now he is more forthcoming. His mother and father don't know what to make of the books. They don't have the basic knowledge or education to ask the right questions. But Jesus looks and speaks like some one who has traveled. So maybe he might have some insights about Archimedes' and Democritus' work.

"I got these books from a Roman soldier who was stationed in Siracusa, Sicily. Archimedes lived and died there. This is a copy of the original book of his private notes. The Roman translated some of the book for me. He also explained as much as he could of the methodology that Archimedes employed to arrive at his conclusions. We met by chance, but he took an immediate liking to me. It was as if he looked at me and I at him and we reached an understanding. It's knowing someone by their gestures rather than by what they say or don't say. So he told me,' I got something that you might like'. Then he pulled these books from his backpack."

Jesus asks, "Where did you meet this soldier? What was his name ?"

"About a month ago, I was playing by the main road when he was walking by. He said something about my solitary game showed some spark. He said he was drawn to me and then he gave me the books. He translated some of it. I asked him some questions. And then he left. His name was Giordano Bruno."

"May I see the books?"

"Sure. Here they are. Do you read Latin?"

Jesus nodded, "Yes."

Archimedes' book was small. The cover and the title and some of the introductory pages were missing. It was wrinkled and a little soiled. But it was in reasonable shape considering that it was an old publication which was being used by a fifteen year old on a daily basis. The book and its binding had a heft that suggested that it was originally an important and expensive publication. Jesus leafed through the pages. One page had a sphere inside a cylinder. Underneath the picture was the explanation: *A sphere has 2/3 the volume and surface area of its circumscribing cylinder.* There was another page showing how to start fires aboard enemy ships using multiple mirrors at different angles. Another illustration demonstrated how to determine the weight or density of objects. It was accompanied with an explanation: *Any body wholly or partially immersed in a fluid will experience an upthrust equal to but opposite in sense to the weight of the fluid displaced.* There were triangle, parallelograms and parabolas. And then there was the challenging statement: Magnitudes are in equilibrium at distance reciprocally proportional to their weights. Then there was a boast by Archimedes when he spoke of the power of levers, Give me a place to stand and I will move the earth.

The other book was by Democritus. It mentioned Leucippus also. This had very few illustrations. It was more a philosophical speculation about the physical world. The physical world it talked about was at the smallest levels. It presented "atoms" as the basic building blocks of all matter. The atoms at the smallest level resembled the collections of atoms at the greatest accumulation. An example included a description of iron. The smallest piece of iron had the same qualities as a sword made of iron. Democritus also theorized that the earth and the universe were a collection of different atoms. There was no pattern or plan for the atoms. They just encountered themselves in the great void of space and in a haphazard manner formed hybrid entities. As proof of his hypotheses, he would study weathered structures. He would find in those bodies different particles of a disparate make up. Democritus also speculated that every person receives a different experience. He said, *"And again many of the other animals receive impressions contrary to ours and even to the senses of each individual. Things do not always seem the same. Which then by the impressions are true and which are false? It is not obvious. For the one set [experience] is no more true than the other than the other but both are alike. There is either no truth or at least it is not self evident."* This book was not what Jesus' work was about. He didn't think the child was possessed. But the woman and her husband wanted some words of comfort or advice.

Jesus said to Isaac, "This book covers a subject that I am not familiar. But I can say this Isaac. Try to do things that you can share with others who are less fortunate than you. Work for the common good. Most people won't know what this book is about. They won't understand what you are talking about. So to be of help and to have more friends you should be more common. You can still enjoy the book. But it should not be your main focus."

Isaac looked into Jesus' face with a look that could have made the Medusa recoil." I have no interest in being popular. Nor do I want to share. Why should I put myself out for strangers? You do speak some truth. Although you do so not intentionally. I will explain. My Roman soldier friend told me of Archimedes fate. Archimedes was killed by a common Roman soldier who was cutting off the sun's light. That complicated an open air experiment that was being conducted by Archimedes. The master told the Roman soldier to step aside and get out of the suns light. The soldier took offense and drove a spear into the chest of Archimedes killing him instantly. What do you think Jesus? Should I waste my time trying to befriend the smugly crude and live a long and dull life at their low level? Or should I truly enjoy liberating, mathematical concepts and apply them to my own well being let the chips fall where they may?"

Jesus asked, "Isaac do you believe in God?"

"Why should I?"

Jesus answers, "Because he is the creator of all things."

"Jesus do you believe the Book of Genesis?" Without waiting for an answer, he asks, "Do you think the earth was created in six days?"

With a somewhat blush, Jesus says, "I never really thought about it."

Isaac pounces, "Democritus would say that any structure as big as the earth would take many, many years to evolve. According to his atomic model the earth is a complex construction of many elements that happened to meet by chance in the original void. They grew close to each other to form other hybrid elements. I understand you have visited India."

"Yes. I have visited India."

"Democritus did also. Did you see the huge mountain range in the north? They call them the Himalayas?"

"Yes I saw them. I have visited Buddhist monks in that area."

"Do you think those great mountains were created in a day? Do you think that the weathering of those mountains show traces of their component ingredients?"

"That doesn't interest me. I am interested in helping people and getting other people to help also."

Isaac replies, "Well I am interested in helping myself. Do you think I could go through life without your help or without the help of Buddhist monks?"

"Probably. But it would also be a solitary uncharitable experience. Other people must be included in the wealth and well being that you would enjoy."

"Who says that?"

Jesus replies, "I say it. I am a witness to the beneficial contagion of good works. Do good and good will be done to you."

"So what bad do I do?" asks Isaac.

"Isaac, you must actively give away things to others in need. "

"Why should I teach others to rely on others? Those are bad habits."

"All people are equal in Gods eyes. We do Gods work by sharing equally. "

Isaac objects, "We are not equal we are known by our difference. By the way, would you help me if I asked?"

"Yes of course, I would help you."

"Good Jesus. I'll let you know if I need you. Good day Jesus."

Jesus was very impressed with the young, wise wordsmith. Once Jesus was a young, wise wordsmith. What was that old saying — Wisdom can be heard from the mouths of babes — thought Jesus. Jesus motioned to his mother to follow him outside. "Good bye Isaac."

Outside of the house and out of Isaac's hearing Jesus tells Anne, "Your son is not possessed by a devil. But he is possessed by self interest. While certain amounts are necessary he has a bit too much. Encourage him to do things that can be understood and shared by others."

Jesus left. Later that night Anne told her husband of the experience. The next day Anne's husband told his friends how Jesus saved his boy's life by exorcising a devil. And that's how Jesus cured the boy. One country-bumpkin's miracle is another country- bumpkin's humdrum. What person or persons who were visited by a celebrity would not embellish the experience?

Chapter VII
Mary Magdalene and Jesus

t was late afternoon in Jerusalem. Jesus was in town. Many knew him by sight. They would greet him or nod with a smile. A lot more men were now wearing their her short and their faces were clean shaven. They picked up on Jesus' new look. Some of those look alike didn't acknowledge him. But they didn't have to, because their hair styles already did. The town was hot and dusty as usual. Jesus was thirsty and headed for alfresco dining at the "Fountain Of Rome". It was a popular outdoor cafe that featured a Roman style fountain that had flowing water coming from a dolphins mouth. No other restaurant in town featured that novelty. It was a mystery to the folks how the water flowed. There weren't any pipes visible entering the locations that could carry water. Where was the water coming from?

Jesus sat at table near the fountain. Birds were splashing a bath in the fountain. They were having a wonderful time. Jesus was shaded by a mature olive tree. The waitress was a few feet away. She didn't notice him because she was reading a book. Jesus certainly noticed her. She had pitch black shiny hair. It was short and curly. Her generous breasts almost fell out of the low neckline cotton blouse. The knee length skirt showed off lovely legs that were shaved as per high European style. They were neatly underneath hips that, when added to the waist and then added to the breasts, totaled up to a symmetrical and enjoyable interlude of passive figuring by patrons. There was one strand of large red beads that were almost a choker fit.

She was engrossed in the book and didn't seem to be on the lookout for service to customers. Maybe she figured that her figure would keep customers busy doing mental strip searches and when they were through filling their eyes they would then fill their stomachs. She wasn't going anywhere and neither were the customers. But the book was giving her some trouble. Whether it was a problem with translation or with understanding a concept, Jesus didn't know. But the waitress acted out frustration by alternatively scratching the upper and lower parts of her body.

Jesus spoke, "Miss. May I have some water and fish with some bread please."

She was somewhat startled. She put the book down and came over to the table. She smiled broadly and made sure her parts were gathered up and covered. She said, "Oh. I am sorry sir. I didn't notice you come in. Water, fish and bread, certainly. I'll put the order in right away. We have some fresh fish that you will enjoy. I caught them myself in the fountain over there this morning." She had an infectious laugh that went with her opener.

"What are you reading?"

"It's Homer's Iliad. A Roman soldier gave it to me. We've been dating."

Jesus was surprised, "Homer's Iliad? I have heard about it but have never read it. What do you think about it?"

"It's not what I am accustomed to reading. I was raised on scriptures which are narrowly focused on our religion. But my friend Virgil talks a lot about his foreign travels. He was stationed in the eastern Mediterranean for a time. So he got into that local history about the Greeks and the Trojan war. He brought this book back and now its mine. But Homer's Iliad is a expansive adventure with heroes that are bigger than life. Yet it is told in simple words. Homer draws you in with his simple descriptions of classic eternal struggles. But I wonder how credible he is?"

Jesus asks, "Why do you doubt his credibility?"

"Well I ask you. Do you think that Agamemnon, Achilles or Hector ever ate in a restaurant? Did those heroes ever take a walk in the country? Did those heroes ever struggle with being misunderstood? Of course they did. But why doesn't Homer tell the stories of the great characters in human terms. Suppose one of histories great characters came into this restaurant on my shift. How would Homer have portrayed my encounter with him? Probably would not have mentioned it. But what about the many readers who don't think in classical themes when going to a restaurant and ordering lunch? There are a lot more people interested in what's on the menu and what did Agamemnon order rather than what Zeus or Aphrodite were up to in the behind the scenes actions. I'll bet you lunch on that."

Jesus is entertained. He hasn't heard breezy, honest happy conversation in a long time. "What is your name?"

"My name is Mary Magdalene. There are so many Marys around. You can see the problem. What's your name?"

"My name is Jesus."

"Oh so you're Jesus. I've heard about you. My friend Isaac mentioned he met you at his home some weeks ago."

"You know Isaac. That kid is brilliant. He talks fast but the ideas and subject matter are a strong concentrated dose."

"I know exactly what you mean. We have long discussions. You may not believe it. But I have a mathematical mind. Isaac picked up on that immediately. We started talking regularly and it's so much fun. It's difficult finding people who speak your language. If you know what I mean?"

"I know exactly what you mean. A simple uncomplicated friendship with any species or ambiance is heaven on earth."

"Now you sound a bit like Homer. No offense Jesus. I'll tell you a secret. But promise me you won't tell a soul."

"I promise not to tell anyone."

"You see that fountain. Do you know how the water keeps flowing?"

"No. I was wondering about that myself."

"Well, that's Isaac's creation. One day I was talking away with Isaac about many things like we normally do. And I was complaining about how slow business was. I thought we needed a novelty to attract more customers. Well out of the blue Isaac suggests that we put a Roman style fountain in the courtyard. It would be attractive to look at and the water would cool the immediate eating area. The Romans would enjoy a little bit of Rome that was recreated in dusty Jerusalem. So I said, great. Let's start working on an aqueduct today. He said that wasn't what he had in mind. He asked if I had ever heard of a water screw? I said, Isaac you are a little young to be talking trash like water screwing. Do you hang out with John the Baptist down at that bend in the river? He said no that's not what he had in mind. He said that Archimedes had a machine called a water screw that lifted water. It moved it from a low point to a higher point. It worked in wells and rivers. But the dynamic could be applied to lifting water from a basin to a storage tank and then releasing the water so it flowed back into the basin where it could be lifted out again. The illusion would be infinite water flows but in reality it would the same water just being recycled. Isn't that brilliant?"

"Yes indeed. I don't think he knows the meaning of boredom."

"Are you bored Jesus?"

"Now that you mention it. Yes I am bored."

"How can a good looking well spoken young man be bored?"

"Why do you say I'm well spoken. We only just met?"

"You speak naturally and without form or fear. That means to me that you are accustomed to speaking. And there isn't any better preparation for anything than to just practice it."

"What do you mean I speak without form?"

"You speak with your eyes, hands and posture in addition to words. That is a total communications. I can spot form speakers. These say more by their rigid body and judicial use of words than by the immediate message they are communicating to me. They make me uneasy. They are hiding something. So for as long as they are around I try to find out what they are hiding. It's a game I play. I started it when I was very young."

"Do you think I'm hiding anything?"

"Not now."

"What do you mean 'not now'?"

"You just told me a few moments ago that Isaac didn't know boredom. Obviously to me was that boredom was a burden to you. Why are you bored Jesus?"

"I am bored because I am frustrated. I had a

gathering and gave a speech. I laid out my philosophy. Some were moved by words. Some didn't know what I was talking about. And still others wanted to use my words against me. Isaac has a better life. He looks at things the way they are. He analyzes why they are what they are and then searches the rest of reality for the same dynamic to prove that he got it right. He's not waiting for people to pat him on the back or buy his book. He is his own reason for enjoying life."

"Where do you think Isaac and you differed in your upbringing to account for the difference in happiness?"

"Honestly, I think I am spoiled. Instead of taking Isaac's approach of accepting reality, I try to change reality. Only a spoiled dilettante tries to change reality to suit his pleasure."

"You do have a point. Since you have identified the problem why don't you change your approach and just go with it. I mean go with life as its dealt?"

"I think its too late. Powerful people are after me. They think I threaten their world."

"Gosh. Now I can see how Homer got so popular writing about the huge struggle between man and man and God. You came in for fish and now you are telling me about your approaching doom. All this at the

Fountain of Rome in dusty Jerusalem. Let me get you your lunch."

Jesus thought to himself. He has never talked to any one this way. He should have met Mary Magdalene many years ago. If he had maybe he would have not gone to India. He would not have been exposed to Buddhism. He would not have tried to establish the middle way in the west. Actually the Greeks beat him to that middle way philosophy long before Buddha was born. The Greeks advocated 'Nothing to excess'. That's the 'middle way'. Only a spoiled child like me didn't take the time to make the connection. So now I may pay with my life for being spoiled.

Mary comes back with the food. She has brought extra. She is going to have a bite with Jesus.

Mary speaks, "here it is. I hope you don't mind, I'm going to join you. It's my break time."

"No I don't mind. It looks delicious. I am sorry I got into a dark mood. I promise to lighten up. Here's to Isaac." Jesus toasts with his water.

"I will second that. Here's to Issac. My girl friend has a crush on you. I can't wait to tell her that I ran into you."

"What's her name? Where did I meet her?"

"Her name is Jessica. You never met her personally.

She was at your talk, the one with the sexy torch singer."

"Now I will play your game. Since the first association with me in Jessica's recounting of her attendance at my talk was to mention the sexy torch singer, I will deduce that Jessica is about your age. She is sexually active. Which implies that her hormones rule her focus more than her mind does. She mostly remembered the sex symbol rather than recant what I spoke about. And yet she has a crush on me. So her motivation must again exclude my talking points. If we take the torch singer reference together with a crush on the personal Jesus rather than speaking Jesus that can only add up to a sexual attraction to me. Am I wrong?"

Mary Magdalene blushes and lets out her infectious laugh, "Boy you're smart."

Jesus answers, "She's having fun and she is honest. Why should she listen to me about the needs of others? That's a bore for her. She knows what her boyfriend wants. He wants the same thing she wants. Give those hormones room to roam. Why trade that real pleasure for some pie-in-the- sky payoff as articulated by a droning spoiled guy who looks bored to death? Here's another toast. Here's to Jessica."

Mary lifts her glass, "Here's to Jessica."

"I have news for you Mary Magdalene. The

combination of people trying to kill me and that coupled with my meeting you, I can report that am no longer bored. I am now happily in the camp of Isaac, Jessica and of course you. From now on I will welcome reality and not try to change it. I will accept life's fortune as I accept the weather. I will dress for it. Here's to life. And here's to the Greeks. Nothing to excess. And no more moping for me." Jesus lifts his glass.

"Bravo Jesus, welcome. But what about us Jesus?" asked Mary. She didn't know what Jesus had in mind with his toasting their meeting. She had been around enough panting hounds to know when they were on the prod. But if Jesus was looking for sex, he certainly didn't make it known.

"Us? Well we just met and according to the Greeks that leaves a lot of room before we experience excess. But for now we are like children. Getting to know each other and enjoying the moment. That will last longer than the carnal. They even have a Greek reference for that. It's called a Platonic relationship. It would seem that the Greeks have not only said it but mostly they have done it also. Isaac was correct when he surmised that indeed there is a master plan but he wasn't sure that a master went with it. He also noted correctly that with the built in design for constant change in the master plan it certainly raises the legitimate question whether the whole life experience is merely haphazard. "

"Are you the Messiah? Jessica would be very mad if I didn't ask that question."

"No. I am not the Messiah. That was the idea of the producers. What did Jessica say about her boyfriend's opinion of me?"

"His name is James. He thought you were clever with an eye to getting involved in politics. According to him your 'pitch' about trusting in God was a fraud. You were, according to him, misleading the average person about the value and need for work. Is he right or almost right?"

"It's not what I meant. But if that's what he said then that must be true. People are listening or better they are hearing what they want to hear. They want more. They figured no one would be in the entertainment business if they didn't entertain or make their audience feel good. So there I was talking about shared sacrifice and most were hearing 'share' and hearing 'sacrifice'. Truly I am naïve."

"Jesus, don't be too hard on yourself. You meant no harm. You spoke what was in your heart about your life's experiences. You honestly believed in their merit.

So if you are misunderstood, whose fault is that?"

"Its their fault but I must pay the price. Let's stop his kind of talk. I want to forget the trouble that I am in. Somehow I think I will get by with just a life's lesson learned the hard way. So what else is new? Right? Say, where do you live?"

"I live on Goliath St. It's number 4 ½ and in the back. It intersects David St. Do you want to visit?"

"Maybe I will. I may need a friends place to hide if things spin out of control. Have you lived in Jerusalem your whole life?"

"I will tell my Roman friend Virgil that I want to end our relationship. So feel free to show up anytime. Have you ever had a real friend?"

"No. I want you as a friend. One true friend is worth more than the acclaim of thousands. Being a popular public figure is a trap. You start the career because you want to express yourself. You want to make a positive difference in people's lives. You are sincere. If you are successful people will demand more and more performances. That will attract more and more crowds. Little by little your performances crowd out other parts of yourself. Until finally you seek refuge from success and seek the right of private self expression. It's the old challenge of moderation again. It really gets to be too much when you find yourself trivializing your message by becoming a cartoon character. "

Mary asks, "What do you mean by a cartoon character?"

"That happens subtly. The necessity of more and more appearances about the same subject matter tends to make stale the whole experience. It turns into something that is akin to a long running stage play. Where the most eloquent thoughts become commonplace because of their repetition. I am so, so tired of being profound. It becomes a creeping, choking vine on my soul. I can't smile as much lest I lose credibility. It's awful. And then people want some new material. But my message and philosophy don't scale up. It's a private affair. And a lot of people don't feel comfortable with themselves when they are alone. They want personal guidance and company."

"OK. That's settled then. We are a pair. But for both of us it's first. We are true friends." Mary leans over and kisses Jesus on the cheek. He clasps her hand and has a look of relief in his eyes. It's as though he has now arrived in a safe port after a long and lonely voyage."

She continues, "Yes, I have lived in Jerusalem my whole life. I content myself to meet men from different places. It's the best I can do. A single woman can't travel alone. So they tell me about themselves. I learn about places that I will never see. But the interludes are quick and over. I am lonely also. But now I am not alone I have you. "

"Have you ever heard of a kite?"

Mary perks up, "Yea. It's that thing on a string that is carried on the wind."

"We are going to get a hold of Isaac. He is going to build one for us three to enjoy on the weekends. That favorite book of his that Archimedes wrote had a kite experiment described. I think Archimedes could somehow tell something important by the length of shadows. And a kite could be used to demonstrate that theory. I am sure Isaac will feel very pleased to explain Archimedes to a couple of country kids. We will be attentive so Isaac gets his full measure of gratitude. We need a carefree day. Get in touch with him. I'll buy a picnic lunch and we will make a grand day of it. What say you?"

"Gee. That sounds great. Just the three of us. Isaac will be so happy."

The day of the kite came quickly. Isaac worked non stop on the project. It was shaped somewhat like a Roman shield. It had a red field with a large "A" painted in white. The "A" stood for Archimedes. The tail was extra long to give it stability. Jesus met Isaac and Mary at her house. They walked a short distance to the edge of town and launched the kite. It was a perfect day for flying. The westerly was gusting and the skies were clear. If there were any problems, one would have to bring them. Right now nature was doing its best just being natural.

Jesus and Mary were more child like than Isaac. They giggled and chattered about nothing and everything. Not one topic was quotable. It seemed by unconscious design that any thing that required more than a second to understand was avoided. And most statements didn't need a reply. It was as two birds chirping back and forth. Lighthearted approach was the rule. And don't break the rule. Occasionally Isaac would break the spell by speaking at length about various Archimedes theorems that were tied to the shadows that the kite made on the ground. Mary and Jesus nodded their appreciation for those facts. Isaac was happy to be the tutor to the adults. He thought how wonderful it could be if his parents could be as happy and frivolous as his two friends. They were all pals now. Fun combines the tangible and the spiritual. And their spirits soared. They stopped for lunch. But not for long. Isaac relaunched the kite. Mary and Jesus took a stroll and saw the old places with new eyes and enthusiasm. The day seemed short for so much fun experience to be crammed into it. It defied physics. The three pals got red noses and cheeks from the sun. They wrapped up the day and headed for the bistro "Fountain of Rome "for supper. All were hungry and thirsty. Mary led them to a table.

"Order what you like. I am an employee and entitled to a discount for myself. I can blur that to include you two. The boss likes me."

Isaac spoke, "How about some lemonade? I'm very thirsty. A piece of fish with some bread would be all I need. What are you all going to have?"

"I will have some water first then wine with some bread," replied Jesus.

"Like wise for me. I will set the table and get the food," said Mary as she got up.

"I can't remember when I had such a wonderful time. I don't think I ever really had a childhood. My mother doted on me. Special tutor and protecting me from other children and the like. How about you Isaac? Is this just routine?"

"Pretty much so, but you and Mary are very special to me. So today isn't just like any other. Why did you say your mother "protected" you from other children?

That's a peculiar choice of words."

"Did I say that? Yeah I guess I did. Well I guess that's the impression I got. It's a long story Isaac. But that's history. I don't want any more history stopping me from enjoying the present. I'm fed up with being the conscious of the world. Most people don't understand what I'm talking about anyway. I'm not even sure that I understand what I'm talking about. I can't remember whether I came to my conclusions through trial and error or whether I am just some human kind of African Grey mimicking what I hear without giving it a thought?

One thing is for sure. Flying a kite today was a better awakening than a baptism is supposed to provide as per the Scriptures testament. Those religious books don't mention one thing about having fun. It's no wonder that religions start so many wars. Religious types were never taught about having fun. Probably don't know how to have fun. So they make themselves more comfortable by dragging others down to their miserable level. What a gruesome class of people. The Sanhedrin wants to have me crucified. I can sense it. I was trying to help people lighten their loads and the Sanhedrin will have none of it. There's no money or power from a small scale carefree religion. They make me so mad. It's almost enough to make me consider taking up a sword and do some hacking and chopping on that malignant association. Hey that could maybe bring a kind of smile to my face. I don't want to die. I just found how to live. I found you, Mary, and the kite. As a whole that is a metaphor for a well balanced life. Of course I would have to get a job. How about kite repair Isaac?" Jesus joked and laughed heartily.

"Kite repair! I'm in. Jesus you are more fun than some of my friends that are my age. I going to advise them to read less or no scripture and take up more hobbies that are in the outdoors."

Mary comes back with the food, "Look her guys. Food and drinks for my best friends."

Isaac says, "It looks delicious."

"I'll second that. Let me help Mary."

Supper is served. And for a short time no words are spoken. It's time to eat.

Mary breaks the silence, "The cook told me some Roman soldiers were looking for Jesus. He told them that he didn't know of your whereabouts or mine."

"Were they asking about you also Mary?"

"I guess so. This is such a small town and the traditional pass time is gossip. We must have been noticed today. It must be a slow news day for us to be the extra edition. You should contact your friends and ask them for advice and help."

Jesus replies, "I have no real friends except you and Isaac. Peter and John were associated with me just for the opportunity of promoting a religious business enterprise. I think the end is near for me. The irony of this whole part of my life is that I have proven myself a successful Messiah type. The proof is the Sanhedrin vicious response. But more ironic is I never thought I was the Messiah nor wanted to be the Messiah as per my producers plans. But I am guilty of going along with the charade. And more irony includes finding true friends because of acting like the promised one. But in the end I abandon the whole enterprise because of my new two, true friends and a kite experience. If anyone ever wrote this story no one would believe it. My life has come to naught except for you two."

Issac drops his head and grasps the hands of Mary and Jesus to comfort them. Mary looks sad and has a premonition of doom about Jesus. She speaks, "Don't be hard on yourself. You have two friends that love you. And the people that you have touched will remember you. They will write history with your deeds."

Suddenly three Roman soldiers arrive at the table. One speaks, "Are you Jesus?"

Jesus nods, "Yes I am he."

"Please come with us. Roman Governor Pilate wants to ask you some questions in the morning. You will spend the night at headquarters."

Jesus rises slowly and sadly. He leans across the table and kisses Mary and then hugs a standing Isaac. He speaks, "Good night my friends. It's been a wonderful day and I enjoyed the supper. I hope to see you soon."

From then on, events moved quickly. The relationship of Isaac, Mary and Jesus didn't have much more time. The larger issues were like a Greek tragedy and other classical stories played out in proxy amongst a small group of people in an every day setting. Soon Jesus would be dead. And Mary would travel to Ephesus where she lived and died. Isaac would continue studying science and keep in touch with Mary for many years.

Chapter VIII
Peter in Rome

eter never caught that next scheduled boat departure from Tyre to Rome. Pilate had engaged all his resources to catch Peter and bring him to the same end that Jesus faced. Jesus is dead. He was crucified about five years earlier. Pilate fulfilled his promise to Jesus. Some crucifixions take days for the person to die. The bleeding isn't the killer. It's the dehydration that terminates in a ghastly, miserable death. But Pilate intervened and had one of his guards lance the heart of Jesus moments after he was hoisted upright on the cross. Jesus died instantly. The word was out on Peter. He was a highly wanted fugitive by order of Pontius Pilate.

So Peter had to avoid shipping ports and well traveled Roman roads. He finally got to Rome, but he took the long way around. He circumnavigated the Mediterranean. He headed east to Asia Minor, took a left at Ephesus and swung back west to finally arrive in Rome. Peter arrived in Rome shortly after Claudius replaces Caligula as Caesar and Emperor of the Roman Empire.

During his circumnavigation he sought others who had met Jesus or had heard of him. Remarkably there were many who claimed to have met him. Some told stories of miracles that he performed. Peter soon discovered that most of these stories were just tales. His simple proof was that if these stories were true, Jesus had to be simultaneously in two places that were separated by hundreds of miles. Peter didn't have to make up stories about the life and times of Jesus. The common folk did that for him. What was their motive? Perhaps they were bored and wanted to be part of something larger? And talk is cheap. He learned that Pilate had resigned his governorship in Jerusalem some four years ago. It was shortly after the death of Jesus. Pilate was fed up with his position of arbitrating arguments amongst people he didn't care for. Peter heard that Pilate moved to Athens, Greece and joined a traveling theater group. His specialty was being a playwright of light comedies. He was offered a commission to do a farce about man and his Gods by Rome's regional governor. But he declined the lucrative offer with the comment, "Life is a farce, light comedy is an art."

Peter had been living in Rome for the past 20 years. He was a quick study. He caught on to the guiding local philosophy, "When in Rome do as the Romans do". He shaved his beard and his hair was cut short. He wore the latest fashions and picked up more manners than the Romans practiced. He bathed at the public baths and conducted business there also. What was his business? Well that answered depended on who you asked. To the common folk, he was an associate of Jesus. He told them that he was carrying on where Jesus left off. He is an advocate for more rights for immigrants and the naturally born Roman citizen. There was no cost for his advocacy work to the followers. They only had to pledge loyalty and help out when called upon. How could a common person in Rome help? Well he could do what he was originally hired to do by an employer and not grouse about extra work. Peter had managed to get in between many workers and their employers. Effectively he was a labor organizer. Some employers would call him a labor agitator. Peter would intercede between employer and employee about wages and work rules. He would bring peace after a grievance. Many times it was Peter who caused the friction. And then Peter would get compensation in money or barter from the employer who was willing to pay for peace. Rome was doing well then. The labor market was tight and Peter had connections. He could deliver workers or he could make things difficult for employers depending on the waxing and waning of Peters greed.

Peter had church services on Sunday. He would identify meeting places normally by public fountains. He would conduct baptisms. He would reminisce with the faithful about his life with Jesus. His stories grew and grew in the scope and size of his contributions to the spread of Christianity. The word Christianity just popped out of his mouth one Sunday many years earlier. Christianity refers to the baptized Jesus. Henceforth known as Jesus Christ. It is so much easier to make contact with the masses if one just trade marks a brand name like Christianity. Then one need only mention the word and the image and the obligations display themselves in the persons consciousness. Word association has always been with us. Another hat that Peter wore was his connections to public officials. Suppose an employer wanted to expand a business or start a new one. All those regulations at the forum would make things tedious and expensive. But a quick meeting with Peter might shorten up the process. And Peter got paid. How did Peter get a relationship with the various Roman internal affairs bureaucracy? It started many years ago when Peter first got into town. A patrician was approached by Peter about storing up a place in heaven after the patricians death. The patrician only had to make a small contribution to Peter's Catholic Church to qualify. Well the patrician complained about the shakedown to the governing municipal authority. The magistrate determined that Peter had broken securities laws and consumer fraud laws. His reasoning was since Peter didn't own any part of heaven he couldn't possibly sell it. Also the fraud charge was based on a corollary of that non deliverable fact I.E. Peter could not guarantee a delivery of a space in heaven because no one was sure where heaven was. And then there was the bizarre incident when a person who had given money to Peter for a place in heaven received a receipt and thank you note from Peter. The person used the thank you note as a deed of trust. He used the deed of trust as proof of heavenly plot asset. Of course the land didn't show up in a title search. Peter settled with the magistrate.

He promised to cease and desist from further prepos-
terous claims. Peter followed up his pledge with regular "friendship"payments to the magistrate. Peter's
Catholic Church never had another problem from the
city. The patrician who filed the original complaint
was notified of the settlement. He wrote down Peter's
name and address in his address book as some one
who could come in handy in the future if he had to
deal with the local authorities.

For many years now, Peter was keeping company with a widowed Jewess. Her name was Sarah. She
was very good looking and obviously had some cross
breeding working to her advantage in her earlier lin-
eage. She was very wealthy and had many political
connections that went to the very highest Roman ar-
istocracies. She had this uncanny ability or fortune of
marrying rich, old money patricians just before they
died. Some suspected she shortened the odds against
a premature death of a husband by her background in
botany and the study of spiders and snakes. But nothing was ever proved and she so far had a string of three
deceased husbands in a row. She was older now and
the crop of old, monied patricians were getting smaller
by natural death before she could get a hold of them.
Peter and she would spend long hours talking after

dinner. They would swap stories over cherry flavored grappa. Their laughs left them gasping for air over recanting past victories. One got the impression that they were laughing at someone and not with someone. Did Peter laugh about Jesus?

And so a new unexpected turn of events would shape Rome and its empire for years to come. Julius Caesar, who claimed a family connection to Prince Aeneas of Troy, gave little thought of the extreme consequences of his crossing the Rubicon. How could he foretell that when he declared himself Caesar and put the Roman Republic at his disposal that a degenerating fate was coming to the empire because of his reckless behavior. No one but Brutus and a few others were outraged enough to assassinate Caesar for his crime. But it was too late. Augustus took his place and then Tiberius and then Caligula and now Claudius. But these all-powerful Caesars couldn't protect Rome from the rot that came from within. The network of roads that carried the riches of the known earth to Rome also carried the rot that comes from inherited wealth. The abundance of empires in the early days do not prepare the following generations for the inevitable decline of sprawling empires. The extravagance of the Caesars was copied by the citizens and the hangover of excesses soon caught up with everyone. Also the people of the far flung empire used the same Roman roads of conquest to mount a counter attack of sorts. They challenged the powers in Rome with, "You have won. But what will you do with us now? Eventually you will go back home?"

The republic is in name only. The Senate and the magistrates and the old line ruling families rule in a de facto plutocracy. Their children didn't inherit a work ethic. They only inherited money and vast land holdings. Consequently they were like babes in a cradle to the likes of women like Sarah. All she did was flatter the old fools and be sexually available to the richest targets. With her insect's heart and mind packaged in the frame of a strikingly beautiful, rather tall, blue-eyed blonde Viking appearance, the patricians were doomed to her wishes. The hybrid that sprang from the cross breeding of the desert species with the northern European species would undo Caesars victories. Sarah had only been around for about 55 years and only 20 of those years in Rome. But she was now the beneficiary of Roman conquests that were the result of over 800 years of works and deaths of the best Roman youth could produce. Peter lacked looks, but he was able to tap into that Roman decadence by promoting democracy and religion driven equality. Rome and its offspring provinces were doomed because of the equality myth. It was certainly "easy go" but it wasn't "easy come" for the ones who earned it. The race to the bottom was on.

Success attracts imitators. And so one day Peter was finishing up a two hour lunch with a wealthy patrician just down the street from the Forum. Peter was making inquires about buying some space for a combination office and place of worship. He needed a corner site. Then worshipers who were entering the building on one side wouldn't see business people entering in the other side. A common wall would separate the interior. The patrician had left. Suddenly two men in a cheeky fashion pulled up two chairs and joined Peter without an invitation. Peter was startled. He left a tip and put the rest of his money in his purse in a hurried way. Maybe these guys were thieves? The two intruders were both in there thirties. They were dressed impeccably and were scanning the surroundings to see if they were noticed by anyone. Peter felt fear.

The heavier and taller of the two spoke first, "Good afternoon Peter. May we join you? My name is Linus and this is my friend Anacletus. We work for large property owners in Tuscany. We would like to discuss some business with you."

Anacletus nodded his greeting to Peter and then spoke," I keep African Greys myself. Aren't they wonderful pets? They listen to what I say. And then they say what I say. But they get bored easily. I get bored easily when I don't get my way. I honor their friendship by protecting them and giving them support and entertainment any way I can. Linus and I have many strings of support that we can pull to help our friends." Anacletus looked for Peter's reaction and then glanced to Linus to nod he had found in Peter's face the look he came for.

Peter was shaken. His face clearly reflected that. Nervously he asked, "What of my African Greys? Are they alright?"

Linus answered, "Certainly Peter. They will be returned to your home tomorrow afternoon. We took them for ride in the country. They didn't mind a bit. They understand when some one who knows how to handle birds is tending them. They enjoyed the change of scene. You should spend more time with them."

"What do you want?" asks Peter.

Anacletus answers, "We want to become your partner. We don't want something for nothing. We are willing to make an investment in your labor relations and religion business. We are already in the political influence field. What do you say?"

"What kind of investment?"

This time Linus responds. It's like a sinister game. One talks then the other. It's clearly meant to intimidate. "We will give you protection from the authorities. We will assist you in organizing laborers up and down Italy. We will also contribute a substantial Roman villa complete with servants for your use as long as you are alive. Also, we would like to manage you and your religion. We want to help you get to the next level."

"I already have protection from the authorities. They leave me alone. You offer management? I am the impresario that managed Jesus Christ and got his religion off the ground. I am all set thank you."

"Regarding protection from the authorities, that's history," says Anacletus. "The authorities are in fact us. We thought you were only making so much. And we were happy with the chump change you gave on a monthly basis. But now we find out that you are making 5 times 'so much'. So that's why we are here. We don't want to shut you down because you and your message look like the future of the Roman Empire. Our families have large holdings in Tuscany and other parts of Italy. They want a hedge against any possible future revolution that your religious/political philosophy might usher in. In short, we want to manage your followers expectations. To do that we want to be part of your church. We want to do this in a business like and friendly way. But make no mistake we want to manage and have a share of your business. You can retain 50% of your present business. But you get only 20% of all new business. There are too many new mouths to feed that's why you have to cut back. Of course 20% of something huge is better than 100% of nothing and a one way ride into the country. "

"How did you find out I was doing so well?"

Linus answers, "Sarah talks a lot. Plus she gets a piece of the action of our new partnership with you. You can't hear every thing Peter. Particularly hard is pillow talk to catch. Sarah gets around. I don't think she sleeps much either. She's very greedy. "

Peter is dropped-jawed. Sarah knifed him in the back. Linus and Anacletus and the powerful network they represent make Jerusalem's Sanhedrin look like little rascals.

"What else do you want?"

Anacletus answers, "We want you to make a will. Nobody lives for ever. We want you to designate Linus and me as your successors in the church of Jesus Christ. Whatever mummery is required, you do it. We will record the will. You will circulate the contents of the will by personal contact to your agents so they know what will happen when you die. There is no rush. Do this at your leisure. We do not want to upset your network of followers. They are the business. I would happily inherit and take good care of the African Greys if that is a concern. You can't trust Sarah. You can trust our word. What say you.? Are you in?"

"Who is your boss?"

"His name is not important. Remember Brutus?"

"Did he and some others assassinate Julius Caesar?"

"Very good, you know your history. Well our boss collaborated with Brutus on that job. You might say that our boss instigated the killing. He didn't believe in Caesar's dream of empire. He liked things the way they were. But Caesar wanted more. And that more meant less for our families' interests. It would have upset the balance of power of local politics. That's history now, but the result of empire has made local politics a lot more fluid. You for example come to Rome and claimed equality. Only an outsider who is a moron would claim equality in the middle of an empire that's run by ruthless plutocrats. Do you know how close you came to being killed the first week? But my family's head was intrigued. He said, 'What's this moron know that I don't know?' So we have been following your movements. That patrician real estate broker that you just had lunch with actually works for us. So we notice that the head count in your religion is going up, we calculate that within a short period of time you may have a significant critical mass of followers to qualify as a constituency. At that point the members in the Senate who are out of power would approach you about wanting your support. We want more than that. Like I said, we want to manage you and your followers expectations. We will bring you all along at the proper time. What do you say to the inevitable? "

"What kind of investment and management do you want to provide to Christ's religion?"

"The clothes you wear are pretentious. Everyone knows you are a Jew from the sticks. The more you try to hide it the more attention you draw to yourself. Embrace your culture. We understand that it isn't much. But that's all you really legitimately have a right to. Give those high Roman fashions away. We can set you up with tailors that can cut you traditional Jewish clothes in a more stylish fashion. Let your hair grow a little more. Wear and trim a light beard regularly. Own some tasteful baubles, bangles and beads. Now some instructions for the church. We want a hierarchy that is dressed accordingly. Nothing splashy but in good taste. Each rung up in the church rule should be correspondingly shown in the clothes worn. If you don't take yourself seriously how will others know to take you seriously. Simple clothing won't be noticed. You have to have a 'Hey look at me outfit'. The church will need to be furnished. It will have to convey a mood of seriousness. We suggest you will need some statues of honored members of your religion. We have controls of guilds that paint and sculpt. Part of the proceeds of our business will be spent on art works. Only designated artisans will work on the projects. The cost of the furnishings and artworks will be paid out of the general receipts before we split up our shares. Do you understand?"

"I understand." says Peter sheepishly.

"Do you accept our generous offer? Do you want to be a member of our family's business? "

A deflated Peter nods approval. Linus and Anacletus get up and leave. And from that time forward the Jewish founded Catholic Church never again had a Jewish pope. The church would only have Italian popes or designated popes influenced by powerful Italian families. Linus followed Peter as pope and Ana cletus followed Linus.

Pontius Pilate would probably hear about Peter and the church and the Italian families moving in. It would most probably reinforce his belief that, "Life is a farce and light comedy is an art." Pilate would be glad to be out of politics and government duties.

Chapter IX
Holy Roman Catholic Church Franchise

he relationship of Peter and the powerful Italian family is working well. Over the years, the church has grown in membership. Also its power has gone viral. The reason stems from the very necessary structure of all great empires. Empires need money and they need control. How does an empire get money and control? First there is the invasion and conquest. Then an empire turns to regulations for control and then to taxes for an income stream. Consequently any means to simplify or avoid regulatory hurdles and avoid taxes is sought by the concerned. That's where the church's Italian family's political connections come in. In addition there is the "labor relations" fee for service and the collections for the "poor". They both produce a steady income that's on an upward trajectory. The

church straddles the secular and the spiritual. It has the potential to dwarf the power of the Emperor and the Senate of Rome. It could grow into the most powerful one-stop-seat-of-power in the known world.

But like all endeavors in life, there are bumps along the way. One particular bump was named Saul of Tarsus. He became a threat to the Catholic Church of Rome in a roundabout way. Originally he was employed by the Sanhedrin of Jerusalem. They were responsible for having Jesus crucified. He would gather information on Christians that threatened the Sanhedrin seat of power in Jerusalem. The Sanhedrin wanted to stamp out the influence of the late Jesus Christ. Saul would report Christians to the Sanhedrin who in turn would have them prosecuted as heretics and blasphemers.

That went on for some time until a miracle happened. According to Saul, he was on a business trip on behalf of the Sanhedrin to Damascus some years ago. On the way, a resurrected Jesus appeared to him in the sky. To quote Saul, the visitation went like this, *"Suddenly a light from heaven shone round him and falling to the ground he heard a voice saying to him, 'Saul, Saul, why dost thou persecute me? And Saul said, 'Who art thou, Lord?' And the lord said, 'I am Jesus whom* thou art persecuting.' And Saul trembling and amazed answered, ' Lord what wilt thou have me do?' And the lord said to him, 'Arise and go into the city and it will be told thee what thou must do . . .'"

Subsequent events led to his immediate conversion to Christianity. He stopped working for the Sanhedrin. After that visitation he was baptized and changed his name to Paul. He westernized the name Saul of Tarsus. It's his troublesome dealings as a newly converted Christian that reaches the ears of the Italian family that partners with Peter in the Catholic Church of Jesus Christ in Rome.

It's early afternoon when Linus visits Peter at his villa next to the Forum. The villa is an extravagance. The Italians know how to live. They promised Peter lodgings for life but the villa went far beyond Peter's wildest imaginings. Only Rome's patricians at the highest level lived better than the former humble fisherman from Galilee.

"Good morning Linus. Good to see you. Would you like something to drink or eat?"

Linus did not have time. Business came first. "No thank you Peter. Have you ever heard of a man called Saul of Tarsus? Actually he now calls himself Paul. He was employed by the Jerusalem Sanhedrin before converting to Christianity. Saul did investigations for the Sanhedrin. He wanted evidence about people who threatened the power of the local rabbis in Jerusalem. He quit them and now he freelances for Christian values. He gives speeches and collects money. But we don't get any. Have you heard of this guy?"

"Yes I have heard of him. I think I met him once. Yes. Now that you describe his former duties, I think he was the guy at Jesus' sermon who was taking notes and questioned me about Christ's probable blasphemy."

"What kind of guy is he?" Linus asked.

"I wouldn't trust him."

"Why do you say that?"

Peter answers in a speculative way, "It's nothing I could put my finger on but I got the distinct impression that Paul or Saul wouldn't stop at anything to get what he wanted."

"Oh he's that kind of guy. I know the type. One week he's collecting info on Christians so they could be prosecuted and killed and the next week he converts to Christianity and starts collecting money for poor Christians who never see any money from the charity donations."

"What collections and from where?" asks a greedy Peter.

"He's working the eastern Mediterranean as we speak. My network of intelligence got a copy of this letter that he sent to the Corinthians. Listen to this. This is Paul's letter, *"Now concerning the collection being made for the saints, as I have ordered the churches of Galatia, do you also . . ."*

A startled Peter jumps in, "He's also tapped Galatia?"

Linus answers, "Yeah. I wonder where else? He just got converted and he's putting points on the score board already. He must own a chariot. The guy gets around. If I wasn't going to have him killed, I would recruit him for our team. Let me continue. Where was I? Oh here it is, *"On the first day of the week, let each one of you put aside at home and lay up whatever he has a mind to, so that the collections may not have to be made after I have come. But when I am with you, whomever you may authorize by giving credentials, them I will send to carry your gift to Jerusalem. And if it is important enough for me also to go, they shall go with me."*

Peter screams, "He's sending the money to Jerusalem? That two timing swine. I'll bet he's still working for the Sanhedrin as a mole in the Christian movement in that vicinity."

An enraged Linus asks, "What makes you think

the Sanhedrin are still involved?"

"Nothing happens in Jerusalem without that council knowing about it. If that money was truly going to
Christian charities in Jerusalem, the Jews of the Sanhedrin would confiscate the funds legally. But since
there are no legal actions that we know of, there is
only one conclusion. The money is going directly into
their coffers. They have already figured a way to scam
the Christian movement."

Linus laments, "Aren't people awful?"

"Linus. You must stop Paul."

"Stop him? Or should we hire him?"

"Explain Linus."

"Let's examine what he did. In essence he linked
people with money to people without money. He was
the broker and got a fee. How did he do that? He really didn't. The Roman Corp of Engineers did it. The
roads they laid down enabled Paul to travel to different parts of the eastern Roman Empire. He then
told wealthy people how ashamed they should be with
their abundance while others in the western part of
the roman Empire suffered from a lack of life's ne-
cessities. He sold guilt as a product. It's amazing how
little people think of themselves. A con artist shows
up and tells a story that may or may not be true and

then people give him money. No sweat. If they didn't give him money, he didn't lose anything. He didn't even sweat to come up with a message. The message was yours Peter. You tweaked the message of Jesus to bring guilt feelings to the achievers. Paul used your message coupled with Rome's grid of roads to go into a business that had no overhead. Peter we got to be part of this. We are going to franchise what we have here in Rome and base it on the test model that Paul demonstrated works in the real world. Then we will export it throughout the known world. I have connections in the Corps of Engineers office. I can have our Christian agents accompany engineer work gangs. As new roads are being built, we can spread the word of the new guilt religion. Somebody will always be interested. The poor will listen because they want something for nothing. The rich will listen because they will be scared or feel guilty if they don't respond. We will need licensed agents. I'll bet Paul knows of other freelancers. They will like to partner with us because of our connections. They will answer to us. No money is going to Jerusalem. No money is going anywhere but to us here in Rome. Peter I want you to come up with some license or sign or medallion that are given to our chain of authorized dealers network in the

Holy Roman Catholic Church."

"I've got the perfect symbol. It will be the sign of the fish. We can use a local fish we caught in Galilee as the model. It's called a tilapia. But suppose Paul and the others refuse?"

"I'll make them an offer they can't refuse."

"How are you going to get in touch with Paul?"

"He has already been kidnapped and should be in Rome in a about a week. I'm glad I didn't kill him outright. Everything has changed for the better. Peter this is big. Now we have a business that will last as long as the roads of Rome will last. It's social consciousness sold as a product. I'm going to update Anacletus and my boss about what happened here today. I will bring Paul here when he arrives in Rome. Is that alright Peter?"

"Sure, Linus. I'll prepare a room. Let me know."

Linus leaves Peter's villa. He thinks to himself that the new opportunity could be huge. But it's going to ruffle the feathers of many who are in the pagan religion in Rome and elsewhere in the Roman provinces. The Holy Roman Catholic Church will start competing for donations from many who give to the pagan God vendors. There is only so much money. Maybe he could include barter as well as money as a way to support the church? Pieces of land, jewelry, livestock and wine could be accepted. Maybe the organization could market the bartered goods for cash? That wouldn't interfere with the pagan God vendors. They're too fat and lazy. They just want money in a sack.

A week goes by. Linus receives word that Paul has been delivered to Peter's villa. Paul is guarded by three of the kidnappers. Linus heads for Peter's villa.

Linus meets with Peter, "Any problems with Paul?"

"No. He got in late last night. The guards have him under surveillance constantly. I only saw him. I didn't say anything. I figured only one guy should initially represent the organization. Guys like Paul plot with simple clues they pick up from small conversations. He will have had a nervous night without any of my conversation to ponder. I'll bring him in now. Also Linus, I recognized him. He's the guy who questioned me at Jesus' sermon. He was working for the Sanhedrin then and probably still is working for them as I suspected."

Three guards escort Paul into the room. Paul walks athletically but has a hint of low self esteem or a guilty conscious by his hunched shoulders. They seat him in a chair in the middle of the room. Linus and Peter are standing a short distance away. Paul looks at both. He's trying to determine who's in charge. Then his face shows a recognition of Peter. He thinks 'Where have I seen this guy before?' No clues yet. No one has spoken. Paul is in his early thirties. He has dark curly hair and almost a black complexion. His face has a severe look. Pock marks cover his shaven face. He must have suffered a severe childhood disease. He is short for a Jew. His clothes though dirty are expensive. He wears numerous rings. Some have precious stones. He says nothing. Paul doesn't ask why he is here or who Linus and Peter are. Consequently Linus determines Paul to be cagey, untrustworthy and he has a guilty conscious.

Linus thinks to himself, this guy collects money from strangers? With a face like that? He speaks, "Who do you work for?"

Paul relaxes. The ice has been broken. Now he can attack. "Do you know my name?"

"It's Paul. You were also known as Saul of Tarsus. I can spell those correctly if I have to write your obituary. Who do you work for?"

Paul tenses up, "I work for myself."

"If you work for yourself, why did this letter to the Corinthians direct them to send charitable funds to Jerusalem?"

"My compliments. You are informed. Jerusalem is my home base."

Linus persists, "The letter also mentions the Galatians. Evidently you solicit funds from them also. Who else do you solicit funds ?"

"You know my name. I don't know either of your names. But this other gentleman I have definitely seen before. Please refresh my memory where did we meet?"

Neither Linus or Peter responds. Paul continues, "I was kidnapped by your agents and brought to Rome. Don't you think it would be courteous even at this late date to introduce yourselves and tell me what you want from me? You obviously have the advantage. What are you afraid of? I'm not afraid of your death threat. You could have killed me days ago and hundreds of miles from this beautiful Roman villa. The threat is meaningless because it's premature and reflects how anxious you both are to get me to cooperate. Therefore you think me valuable to your organization. So let's make a deal."

Linus faintly smiles, "You are a clever reptile. I am Linus and this is Peter. You met Peter at a sermon that Jesus gave some years ago. You were collecting evidence against Jesus at the time. You were working for the Sanhedrin. Do you still work for the Sanhedrin? "

Paul answers, "Now I remember. Yes I was working for the Sanhedrin."

Linus continues, "Between the both of us we manage the Holy Roman Catholic Church. The late Jesus Christ was it's founder. Peter worked with Jesus in getting his message out. Now Peter answers to me. We run the day to day operations of the church and plan for its expansion."

"So its about expanding? If I could live like you both do I accept. But for the record what do I have to do and what do you have to offer a prospective employee? "

"You still haven't told me who you work for."

"Part of the time I work for the Sanhedrin in Jerusalem. Part of the time I work for myself. The Sanhedrin doesn't know about my freelancing."

Just at that moment, one of Peter's African Greys screeches," Hail Claudius." Simultaneously the parrot extends his right leg and claw as to salute the Emperor.

Paul chuckles at the bird antics and asks with a sly smile, "Does Claudius know everything you are doing? And you Peter, do you feel any remorse for freelancing on the grave of Jesus? The grave you helped dig? And I heard Jesus speak. He didn't say anything about founding a church. That's your idea." He looked accusingly at Linus and Peter.

Peter drops his eyes to the floor. He is sensitive to Paul's accusation. But Linus coldly stares at Paul and answers with a menacing tone, "People who know too much or think they know a lot can regret it. Those kind of questions and accusations and judgments can make me forget about dirtying a clean Roman villa floor. Do you have any other partners? Do you run a network? What do you sell? To whom do you sell?"

"You want a lot of information. And I will tell you. But do I have any guarantees that you won't do away with me after I tell you all you want to know?"

Linus takes one step towards Paul, "You can be valuable to this organization. You have demonstrated talent in setting up a charitable donation business. We have the same business model here in Rome and throughout Italy. We can open new markets to you through the organization's connections in the Roman Empires political network. What we are looking to do is create an umbrella franchise of the Holy Roman Catholic Church. We want people like you to work with us in developing new markets. We want to standardize the business. From the pitch to the collection to the payouts to the protection of our employees, together we can be more profitable and secure. With the organization behind each individual franchise holders territories, there will be no danger of poachers moving in. Because we know how to deal with poachers.

Look at you. You are an example of how we work. We hear everything and we have long arms. What do you think? Are you in?"

"What happens when the Sanhedrin finds out that I left for another employer?"

Peter answers, "Linus can handle the Sanhedrin. He is a man of his word and has considerable muscle to back it up. As you know I worked with Jesus. I developed his public persona and identified the people who would be interested in his philosophy. I can help you and other franchise members with marketing. Do you have any other people involved in your particular markets? And what markets do you cover? And for the record, do you believe in God."

"Nobody ever did anything for me. So I only believe in my abilities. The Sanhedrin reassigned me to be an undercover operative for them in the Christian movement. They wanted information on the network for later prosecutions. But then they added this collections business because they couldn't resist free money. Aren't they awful? After I got their plan up and running, I cut myself in. I recruited others and expanded on my own. Some of the collections did go to charitable causes but most contributions didn't make it out of our pockets. May I comment on your original advice to Jesus about altering his message to include a soak the rich and all are equal philosophy?"

Peter answers, "Certainly."

"With all do respect, you can overplay those two ideas. Our best and most honored customers are the rich. We can't insult them. Either by telling them they owe the fruit of their labors to unknown recipients. Also this equality nonsense. How are going to build anyone's ego whether they be rich or poor if all you have to offer at the end of the day is equality? We as an organization have to subtly flatter our constituency. After all we can only get money from the rich. We can't call them dirt balls because they worked hard. And also to the poor we have to advise them that our charity work is a bridge to self sufficiency. That way we get to use them as workers in our cause rather than passive consumers. I have one associate who has followed your original pitch religiously. His name is James. He works Jerusalem undercover. He is abrasive. I heard him one day talking to a small group of wealthy merchants. And I quote, *'Come now, you rich, weep and howl over your miseries which will come upon you. Your riches have rotted and your garments have become moth eaten. Your gold and silver are rusted and their rust will be witness against you and will devour your flesh as fire does. Behold the wages of your laborers who reaped your fields which have been kept back by you unjustly . . . '* Then he adds more insult by accusing them of not being charitable enough if their donations don't satisfy him. Peter, if I may be so bold, I surmise that your definition of equality has two meanings. To the poor the word equality means a starting point to a better life. To the rich the word equality means an ending to the life that they worked for. And you are happy to play one off against the other and get paid from both sides as the manager of expectations. That's too crude. It works marvelously in the real world but it carries a long term threat of rot and hate. We can continue to play it that way. But if I had my druthers I would tweak it back to what Jesus had in mind. But that risks the growth of the Holy Roman Catholic church."

Peter says, "You have a point Paul."

Linus asks, "How much were you collecting and what were your territories?"

"I covered the eastern basin of the Mediterranean. I had the help of Timothy of Ephesus, Titus of Crete, Philemon and James is in Jerusalem. All five of us on average collected about 1000 pieces a month in total."

Linus is impressed, "That's a surprising amount. Are you telling me the truth? Why did these people give you, a total stranger, money for people they had never met and for causes that were hundreds of miles away?"

Paul answers, "Yes. The figures are truthful. As for your question about charity and anonymous people and causes, I asked that question myself. The answer is simple. People want to help. They believe what I say that some one needs help who lives a considerable distance away. If it was a closer distance they could check for themselves. So distance is a way to hide the truth. We three think that is stupid for people to give money to charity. But the honest intentions of simple people are the only real facts that we make a living from. Most everything else is false. We know so much more. Or do we?"

Linus focuses on Paul. He wants this part of the conversation to be understood, "We are going to franchise the Holy Roman Catholic Church. Each franchise holder will be given an official medallion in the shape of a fish. Franchise holders will be called bishops. Its from the Greek word for overseer. The franchise holder will have specific areas of operation. And that will be strictly enforced. That's the essence of a well run franchise. Peter is the Bishop of Rome. I am his heir. You will make Peter your heir if you join our family. You will probably be called the Bishop of Galatia. But there will be an extensive chain of overseers. Many you won't know their names or know their faces. But they will know you. And they will answer to me. Books will be kept. And I assure you, you will be watched. Count on that. There will be no more private entrepreneurship. Any deviation from our system of bookkeeping and territories will result in immediate termination. And that means you wont do anything for anyone anymore and that includes yourself. Do I make myself clear?"

Paul answers, "You do. What is in it for me?"

"Your loyalty to us will provide for you a life long security relationship. Peter's villa was provided by our organization. He retains 50% of his original business income and receives 20% of all new business. The same deal is being offered to you. We will build you a church. It will have ample living quarters for you. You will have personal protection if necessary. Our connections here in Rome will assure you a trouble free relationship with the law. All you have to do is take our orders and do not ask questions that you don't have a compelling reason to know. "

Peter asks Paul, "What do you think of Christianity?"

"My cynical opinion is that Christianity can be a

business that puts buyers and sellers of guilt together. My gut opinion is different. My gut tells me it has validity. Helping people is natural. Trying to make a business of helping people is unnatural. Personal good will and charity doesn't scale up to an institutional size without a lot being lost in the process. In short people game the philosophy. Whether it be donors who are trying to buy peoples good wishes. Or whether it be receivers who rely on charity to avoid work. And then there are people like us. We are the middle men who broker guilt for a profit."

A concerned Linus asks, "Do you have your heart in this project or not?"

"I do. But I also believe in giving value. We will profit. I guarantee that. But I would want this franchise to deliver some of what it promised. I don't want to excessively rip off people. We should provide schooling. We should talk about law and order. Hygienic living conditions and habits should be encouraged. We want to be part of the community at a wholesome level. If we are going to be thieves, we won't last long. To build for the future we have to be perceived as giving back value to the community."

Linus speaks, "Interestingly put. I'm going to think about what you advise. It makes sense strategically. Do you sell any products or do any fee for service business?"

"We do a lot of circumcisions. Do you want to help Linus?"

"What else?" snarls Linus.

"Some animal sales for offerings. Some match-making in arranged marriages. A little counseling and hand holding. Don't underestimate the income that our church can reap by helping others to sooth their guilty conscious. Also I charge for baptisms and wedding services. It all adds up. I accept all kinds of payments. Barter is welcome."

"I'm curious. Barter intrigues me. I was thinking about that form of payment a while ago. It relates to the availability of coin of the realm and other competing charities. How do you convert to money?"

"I have a chain of dealers who I deal with in bartered goods. Some move live animals for me. Some move donated food. Some move donated clothing. You get the idea. The key is preparation. Have a disposal network in place before you get the odd donation. Then you can honestly smile when they hand you a basket of apples. You have to maintain a pleasant and thankful attitude. After all I approach someone who doesn't know me and ask for a donation so I can help people who are far away and is unknown by the donor. I can't ask for specifics. I have to be ready to receive generalities and be thankful for it. You have to service the customer.

Linus likes the way this guy thinks and operates. And yet he looks like a reptile! The positive message of charity over comes his negative physical looks. That is key. "I like your style Paul. You may have additional duties as a troubleshooter for the organization."

Paul replies, "I don't mind working. But I like to be paid a fair compensation."

"Ask Peter if he has any complaints about wanting for anything? I want you to contact those associates of yours and set up a meeting here in Rome with me and Peter and some others who will help you with your network needs. Also you will right a will. You will be part of our family and as such any of your possessions will be left to our family business. You will leave your possessions to Peter the Bishop of Rome. As I said earlier he has me as his heir. The family wants the temporal and the spiritual assets separated for security reasons. If we lose a civil war then we would suffer a loss of personal properties. But we would still have the church's assets and vice versa. You will live like a king but your title will only be bishop."

Paul answers, "Very clever. So be it. I leave everything to Peter."

Peter speaks, "Tell me Paul. What about this miracle? What about this visitation of Jesus to you when you were traveling to Damascus? Is that true?"

"I don't know."

Peter looks confused, "What do you mean you don't know. Did Jesus appear to you or not?"

"It's this way Peter. Remember your partner John talking about the drug soma? Well I remember his description of its mind expanding powers at the sermon. I also got a hold of his Apocalypse prediction papers. It makes for wild reading. Never read anything like that before. Shortly after that I bought some and tried it. He was right. It changed me forever. But occasionally I get these same soma experiences without taking the leafy potion. So that's how I saw Jesus. I guess I was lucky. But I honestly don't know whether it was him or the drug."

Peter asks, "What do you think Jesus would say about the Holy Roman Catholic Church Franchise?"

"Don't fret Peter. By comparison the bishops who follow us will make us look like saints."

Chapter X
Peter Receives A Letter From John

eter has done well in Rome. Things have moved quickly. The success of the Holy Roman Catholic Church has surpassed his and Linus' greatest hopes. The church regularly receives donations of all kinds. Included is land, jewelry, paintings, sculptures, livestock, and food of all sorts. Initially Peters villa was the repository of the valuable collectables that were donated. But his villa was not equipped or big enough to house the increased flow of valuables nor the livestock and food that was offered. Consequently ground was being broke on a much larger facility. It was to be a church building that rivaled Rome's massive public buildings. Peter and his associates had to set up a sophisticated logistic system of receiving goods and then distributing them to the needy. If you offer something

for free people will come and accept it. No surprise there. The sinners gave to ease their conscious and to get political and religious indulgences and the needy happily relieved the sinners conscious by taking the food off their hands.

The explosive success of the Catholic Church attracted malicious and envious attention from some very powerful vested interests in Rome. Particularly upset is the group that runs the Roman pagan religion. They don't like the attrition of their faithful who are becoming Christians. They also resent the active poaching by the Catholic clergy who dangle equality and social safety nets under the noses of the common Romans. The motley pagan religion was originally set up by an elite class of rulers over thousands of years. They created and crafted the Gods to suit their own specifications. They described them and taught the common folk what the Gods expected. This would manage perceptions and expectations of the believers to the purpose of combining Gods wishes with the ruling class needs.

But the Catholic Church twisted that tradition. They taught there was only one God and that the common folk were the real repository of power who deserved equality in its broadest definitions. That turned the elite religion upside down. Peter reflected on the size of the church and how the personal religion of Jesus doesn't scale up without losing the whole intent of Christ. But it's too late now. Not that he cares anyway. He doesn't believe in God. Nor did he believe that Jesus was the Messiah. He just wanted to get out of Jerusalem. And he did that. Although it was a pity that Christ was crucified. He notices a letter on the table. It's from Egypt. It's from John. It's been many years since he saw him. The last time was at that sermon that Jesus gave. John ran off with the opening act. She was a torch singer and a knockout. What was her name? Nefrateri! Let's see what John has been up to. I have missed him. Peter finds a chair and opens the letter.

"Dear Peter,

It's been many years since we fished in the Sea of Galilee. In some ways those were some of the most happy days for me. In other ways I am glad to be done with them. I have missed you. I heard about Jesus and his gruesome end on the cross. He was a good person who didn't deserve that kind of horrible treatment. What a world we live in. What kind of God designed that fate? As you have noticed by the envelope, I am living in Egypt. I

MARRIED NEFRATERI AND WE HAVE TWO CHILDREN. BOTH ARE GIRLS. MY LIFE WITH THE THREE OF THEM HAS BEEN WONDERFUL. MY CURIOSITY ASKS OF MY FORMER WIFE GEVALTA. HAVE YOU HEARD OF HER? I DON'T MISS HER. BUT I'M STILL CURIOUS.

MY WIFE'S FAMILY GROW WHEAT. I HELP OUT PHYSICALLY. BUT I ALSO HAVE DEVELOPED A WHEAT TRADING AND STORAGE BUSINESS. IT'S BEEN VERY SUCCESSFUL. WEALTHY EGYPTIANS CONSULT WITH ME ON WHEAT AND OTHER GRAINS. SOME GIVE ME MONEY TO MANAGE FOR THEM. I HAVE INVENTED A FINANCIAL PRODUCT BASED ON THE FUTURE PRICE OF GRAINS AND WHEAT. IT'S A TACTIC TO HEDGE AND PROTECT COMMODITY PRICE EXPOSURE. SOMETIMES I "SHORT" WHEAT. IT'S A LITTLE LIKE SELLING SPACE IN HEAVEN. YOU DON'T OWN IT BUT PEOPLE HAVE FAITH THAT IT'S THERE SO THEY GO ALONG WITH THE GAME. OCCASIONALLY MY FAMILY IS INVITED TO WEALTHY EGYPTIAN HOMES FOR ENTERTAINMENT. I FEEL VERY PROUD AND HONORED. I FOUND A HOME. IT'S GREAT TO BE OUT OF JERUSALEM.

WHAT A DIFFERENCE THERE IS BETWEEN PALESTINE AND EGYPT. HERE THERE IS ABUNDANCE. PEOPLE ACT DIFFERENTLY. THEY TREAT EACH OTHER DIFFERENTLY. DON'T MISUNDERSTAND ME. WE ALL SUFFER FROM THE DEMONS OF BEING HUMAN. BUT SOME PLACES ARE MORE

COMFORTABLE TO LIVE. ONLY SOME ONE LIKE ME WHO IS A STRANGER TO EGYPT CAN COMPARE. EGYPTIANS WHO HAVEN'T TRAVELED DON'T KNOW THE DIFFERENCE.

FROM WHAT I HEAR, YOU ARE VERY SUCCESSFUL IN ROME. IN CHARGE OF THE HOLY ROMAN CATHOLIC CHURCH? YOU'VE COME A LONG WAY. RELIGION HERE IN EGYPT IS A RICH MANS GAME. THE PHARAOH RUNS THE WHOLE SHOW. HE BUILD PYRAMIDS AND COLOSSAL COLUMNED STRUCTURES IN HONOR OF THE GODS AND IN HONOR OF HIMSELF. HE BLURS THE CONNECTION. IT SEEMS LIKE HE IS ONE WITH GOD. AT LEAST HE CAN SIT AT THE SAME TABLE IN THE NEXT WORLD. IT MAY BE TOO EARLY FOR A RELIGION LIKE JESUS PREACHED TO GET A FOOTHOLD HERE IN EGYPT. BUT TIME IS ON THE SIDE OF ANY EXPANDING POPULATION. THEY WILL DEVOUR EVERYTHING AND EVERY ONE.

PLEASE PLAN A VISIT. YOU WILL STAY WITH US. I HAVE A FAVORITE FISHING SPOT. WE COULD HAVE FUN.

YOUR OLD FRIEND,

JOHN

Peter puts down the letter. He thinks how well things have turned out for John. Two daughters, a beautiful wife, a supportive greater family, wealthy friends and being accepted and respected all add up to success by any ones measure. And it's all legitimate. No lies, no sensational marketing jingoism and no one gets hurt. I must visit him. I will get a letter off to him soon.

But I have to check my calender of appointments. Leisure time or vacations is a rarity in my line of work. One must be seen to be doing good to maintain credibility. Linus is watching. Linus is hungry. Linus is always hungry for more. He's insatiable. I should know about insatiable appetites. Look at me. My life has gone from a simple fisherman who lived from day to day to a person who accumulates more than I can possibly use, eat or enjoy in ten lifetimes. That is stupid, because people notice and want what I can't possibly use or enjoy. So I am in this trap of protecting my abundance that I can't enjoy. It's insane. I have become a butler in my own house. All my goods come first. Before I can enjoy one single day, I must spend at least half of the day dusting things off, checking for stolen goods, arranging deliveries of more things and weighing every conversation I have to try to determine if there is a plot afoot to take away things I don't really need. Silly, silly, silly.

Sarah really hurt me. I so enjoyed her company. Was there anything sincere and friendly about the whole relationship? Or was she just trying to get inside information about my success at the church? How many real friends does she have? Maybe she is as poor as me when it comes to adding up a column of friends? I would accept her back in spite of everything she did to me. When you are in a desert you drink even foul water.

I know John is my friend. Of course that's not an apple to apple comparison. John and I were both equal when it came to wealth. We didn't have any. That's why we got on. And then he went away. That put him out of harms way from my greed and I was out of his possible greed and envy by the same judgment. Maybe my one and only friend is a result of us being separated? Isn't that a poor comment on my integrity and values? It's all about money. And then when you get it you want more. The price is loneliness, but one gets accustomed to being alone. One compensates by making a virtue of being cynical about everyone's motives. How many possible friends did I turn away by my judicial conversations? Why would anyone think me worthy of the time if all I projected was a cagy greed in my talking? And if I was really sincere about changing my life would I take up the message of Jesus? His message was simple. Do good and good will be done to you. That's not what me, Paul and Linus are really selling in our traveling circus of holy lies and door to door begging.

Would I or could I do it, could I take up Jesus' advice? Throw away all that I have attained and take up the simple life again? I don't think so. My problem goes too deep. My problem is I don't believe in anything. I don't believe in God. I don't believe in friends because I would have more if I did. I really don't believe in money because of its demands. But I cling to it by default. If I didn't have money now, I wouldn't know what to do with myself. You can't do anything with money except make it and spend it. It's a total exercise of banality. But that's the vortex I'm in.

My life as a fisherman offered more drama. I sweated when I fished. It was an honest sweat. Not a nervous money grubbing sweat that requires more energy because of the unnatural nature of pursuing a sack of wealth. Lying to oneself that the pursuit of money is justified no matter what the means. Financial wealth is relatively new to common folk like me. We used to barter for most of our needs. That was better. By definition barter comprised human relationships. Friendships developed. Litigation wasn't a component of barter. Your word was your bond. How simple. How wonderful is that kind of trust. That's better than a magic show. No needs for veils or smoke. Just the truth please.

Let's face it. I am not going to change. I am not built for friendship.

Under different circumstances and another time and place I might have had a more rewarding life. But with the temptation of money I have caved in to some deep seated flaw. It's hopeless. I wonder if I should write John? Maybe it would be more honest just to let him have pleasant memories of our relationship and not let him see what I have become? And what of Sarah? I want her back. I would give anything to have a relationship like that again. And what would I give? I would have to give myself. And that's something I have never been able to do. That's why I always end up with broken dreams. I have to give to get. But I can't cross that initial threshold.

Peter's reverie was disturbed by the entrance of his servant. He spoke, "Master I have news. Emperor Claudius has died. And Nero has replaced him."

"When did you hear this and from whom?"

"It was just announced in the Forum. I heard it myself while shopping."

"Thank you. Please contact Linus and request a meeting here as soon as possible."

A week later Linus arrives at Peter's villa for a meeting. Linus is announced and greets Peter with a worried look. "We have problems Peter. I would have been here days ago but I needed to find out what the policies will be with the new Emperor Nero. It looks like our partners in the Senate and other important contacts in government have been severely compromised and in some cases we are out of effective power for the time being. His allies have quickly moved in to seize the pivotal power points. They were given those slots by Nero in return for their help in giving Nero a free reign in building projects and personal indulgences. Our religious revenue stream was one of the first sources of money identified for Nero's use. They want to shut us down so the pagan cash flows ramp up again."

"Out? You said out? What kind of tactics?" asks an alarmed Peter.

"Yes. It's particularly bad for our religious interests. Nero wants more revenue and he spotted the attrition of pagans in favor of joining our Catholic Church. It's going to get rough for as long as he is in power. We may have to go underground. He can by decree outlaw the Holy Roman Catholic Church. That would dry up the funds immediately. He can confiscate property. You will have to leave this villa and Rome altogether.

I can set you up in the coastal regions just south of Rome. It will be south of Antium. It's by the water and a lot less political than Rome. Nero wont have much of a spy network in place. That could change and then you would have to move again. But you will still be required to be out of sight. If we can lower our profile, we may avoid an outright decree of criminal behavior. And then we could come back another time."

"How can we go underground? We are at our peak right now. We have respectability. We have worked hard setting up the whole organization. We are expanding in the provinces with Paul and his networks help. How can we still operate under cover and survive? Isn't that like committing suicide?"

Linus answers, "It's the next thing to it. We have no choice. We have to have a low profile to avoid Nero's ruthless vengeance. He kills for sport. He's like a greedy kid and he is cold blooded. I'm taking a chance coming here in public view. His spies are every where. We can't meet in public again. Start packing. I will send two of my men to help you move later today. They know where to take you. We have no choice Peter. Survival is the object now. No body knows how long the emperor will live. He could be assassinated today or years from now. Two of our last five emperors were certainly killed. I have heard that Nero's mother Agrippina the Younger may have poisoned Claudius. That would make three of the last five Caesars killed. Claudius made Nero his heir about a year ago. I remember thinking 'Claudius wont be around much longer'. I was right. Such is life in the highest echelons of Roman culture. And Nero looks to be a perfect candidate for a similar fate. But we could get killed ourselves while waiting. Please consider that if they can kill the emperor they can certainly eliminate a former fisherman turned religious guru and his partners."

"I got it. I'll start packing immediately."

CHAPTER XI
The Ponty Pilate Light Comedy Revue Comes To Town

We live irony. It's because there is only one life experience and we all take turns. Peters decamping in haste to the coastal region south of Antium eventually includes a grand example of ironic coincidence. Peter has been settled. It's been five years since he relocated to the greater Antium area. He receives word from Linus. Linus has a dark humor sometimes. He starts off his "be on the lookout" note to Peter by challenging Peter with a question, "Guess who's coming to town?" The letter goes to announce that "It's Pontius Pilate, the former Roman Governor of Palestine will be arriving within the month! Will wonders ever cease? Peter learns that Pontius Pilate is opening *The Pilate Light Comedy Revue* in Antium. It's an out-of-town opening to prepare for a Command Performance before Nero in Rome in

a months time. Pilate carried out the required crucifixion of Jesus which was against his better judgment.
But the law had to be followed. That foul act made Pilate reevaluate his life. He concluded to abandon his
Roman governorship and pursue the arts. It concerns
Peter because as governor Pilate also put out an arrest
warrant for Peter and John that was never carried out.
Peter thinks, "Pilate wanted me when I was the impresario. Now he's the impresario. Now I'm the persecuted
holy man and Pilate couldn't care less. I shouldn't have
sold my fishing boat. Life was simpler then."

He now calls himself Ponty. He has let his hair
grow but it is in a pony tail. He is still clean shaven and
handsome as ever. And his open chested tunic has become the fashion for free spirits everywhere. The stage
productions have been very successful and critically
acclaimed. The show circuit includes the outline of the
Mediterranean from east to west and back again. The
name Ponty symbolizes his new light touch approach
to life and to entertainment. He is the manager and
theatrical director of a repertory group that specializes
in old and new comedy plays. The old plays are largely
revivals of the 4th century Greek, Aristophanes, who
is considered the Father of Comedy. That collection
includes biting and funny social commentaries; *The*

Clouds, The Birds, The Wasps and *Plutus, etc.*

Ponty also writes and produces original works of his own. In fact the world premiere of his Statues will be presented in Antium and then in Rome to Nero. Ponty is famous for opening his performances by reminding the audiences that, "No truly funny entertainer has ever been put to death or been exiled. And I hope that this evenings presentation will continue that tradition. I work hard so I may live and entertain you tonight." In interviews he quotes Aristophanes who famously said, "The author and director of comedies has the hardest job of all." Indeed. Ponty adds, "Life is a farce, but light comedy is an art."

Peter hears of Ponty's schedule. He can't resist attending although the risks are great. Linus was accurate. Nero's network of spies is closing in on him and others of the family of Linus' religious enterprise. Peter will have to disguise himself. Fortunately, the play Statues will be an evening performance. Maybe just a hood will be enough to sneak by? He had a friend buy his ticket. So all he has to do is present the ticket and find his seat.

Opening night arrives. The greater Antium area includes the wealthiest Romans as part of the population. Their country villas are over-the-top in

extravagance. All the beautiful people of Roman society show up for *The Pilate Light Comedy Revue.* He
sees Sarah. She literally elbowed her way to be closer
to Nero's consul Seneca. Peter notes Sarah's all out
effort to graft herself to Seneca. The all out includes
breasts that are almost all out and a hint of perspira-
tion on her forehead from pitching Seneca too hard
on deals. But wise and tasteful Seneca is not buying.

Peter finds his seat. A harp and a lute keep an appropriate tempo and mood for the audience to be seated. The evening is perfect. The late spring air is filled
with the sweet scents of budding flowers. The sky is
clear. People refrain from talk. Those that do, only use
few words in a hushed tone. The men and women are
dressed in their finest. It's Roman culture at its highest level. Quite a sight thinks Peter. They know how to
live. The amphitheater is filled to capacity. The music
stops. And from stage left walks out Ponty. Consorting
with the Muses has agreed with Pilate. He looks better
than when he was Governor in Palestine some 25 plus
years ago. He exudes confidence and self satisfaction
in the best sense. He's is a man at peace. He speaks.

"Good evening ladies and gentlemen. I am Ponty.
Thank you for coming. Tonight will be the world
premiere of my new work "Statues". It's a play that asks

the age old question that is judged by Aristotle as the singular most important question, 'How should one live his or hers life?' Ponty coyly adds, "This is odd because the questions are represented by statues and they don't talk much."

The audience gives out a mild chuckle.

Ponty adds, "No truly funny entertainer has ever been put to death or has been exiled and I hope that this evenings presentation will continue that tradition. I work for my life and for your pleasure. Without further delay, please enjoy the show."

The audience politely clap. The decorated light weight screens that were the backdrop for Ponty's introduction are removed. The stage now shows 3 statues. All the statues are exactly alike. There is nothing remarkable about any of them. They are purposely off center. The purpose is a clue that one statue is missing. Ergo that is part of the plot. An actor walks on from stage right. He doesn't acknowledge the audience. He pauses and proceeds to the first statue. Each statue has a plaque of description.

The actor speaks obliquely to the audience while examining the statue, "Let's see here. This statue's plaque says simply "I am Fame." Oh I get it. That's why this statue has that far away look in its eye. It's not looking where it's at but where it's going." The audience titters. "Does this statue have a broken arm? I think it does. Such is the cost of fame. While working on ones image in the mirror one may miss a step along the way." The audience giggles.

The actor moves to the next statue, "This plaque says "I am Wealth". Gee. It looks similar to fame. The face evokes a holier than thou stare. Oh now I see. Here down at the bottom is a stamp stating the expensive price and that is was paid by the same wealthy patron that posed for the statue. I guess the Wealth figure wanted to drive home the point that the statue was costly but affordable to the plutocrat. It also indicates that it was paid for in cash." The audience laughed heartily.

The actor now acknowledges the audience with a sly wink of appreciation. He then turns next to the last statue. He reads the plaque. He speaks, "I am Religion." Umm. Religion uh? Wait a minute. It's clear now. The look in the eye has a farther away look than Fame and the "Paid "stamp that was on Wealth Statue is missing and in it's place is a sign stating, "Please Donate For Statue Cost. And Inquire Within For Special Low Cost Indulgences." A convenient bucket for coins is provided. The audience roars. Peter laughs so much he gasps for air. He slaps his thighs. He forgets his troubles. The whole audience feels the same way he does.

After a long while, the audience finally compose themselves and resume attention on the stage actor. The actors dead pan had also gave way to laughter. He too composed himself and moved to the last plaque on the stage. That is placed before an empty place where a statue should be. The actor looks around to make sure he's not missing anything.

He says, "What does this plaque say? This plaque reads, 'This Place is Reserved For the Light Of Heart If they Ever Tire of Having Fun.' That speaks volumes. Fame, wealth and religion are a trap. To avoid those popular traps one should at least one day a week follow a butterfly around. You in the audience have behaved like butterflies in attending. Don't become a statue for any reason. Thank you folks for coming tonight. Good night."

The audience sighs wistfully and then vigorously clap. Some stood. Peter stood up and clapped. He was moved. He can't stay longer. Up with his hood over his head and to the exits and to home. This is getting old. His position at the church is not worth the trouble. Linus needs to be told.

Chapter XII
Linus Offers Nero A Deal

inus has his own concerns about the precarious state of affairs of the family's religion business. He reviews the status of The Holy Roman Catholic Church. It's been five years since Nero became Caesar. Peter is still in Antium out of sight. The cost of Peter's seclusion is high. He still draws his share of the income. And his living expenses are more with the added security he requires. But Peter can't be seen in public. So that precludes Peter from working and developing new Christians and the income stream. Linus wonders how he can solve Nero's pressure against the Christian religion and Peter's drag of non-productivity in one motion. Maybe he can meet Nero half way. Give Peter to Nero. Then Nero could claim a trophy on behalf of the pagan religion lobby by executing Peter. With

Peter gone, Linus then becomes a low profile Bishop of Rome protected by Nero. Peter's share of the profit would be given to Nero. That would be money for Nero's personal use. It wouldn't have anything to do with tax collections or bureaucrats. Nero has huge appetites. He is always getting pressure from the senate to curb expenses. This would free him from oversight. Nero could help with disposing of deadbeat Christians. And Linus could help with Nero's problems with unwanted immigration to Rome.

He will have to arrange a private meeting with Nero. The Villanovans are the deep pocketed and politically powerful family that is behind Linus. They predated by at least a thousand years the Julio-Claudian dynasty which Nero is descended. Nero will want to know what the man from Family Villanova has to say.

About a week passes. Linus receives a note from the palace that Nero will see him and please come alone so they may talk frankly. Linus heads to the Forum. In front of the palace's entrance is a colossal 100 foot high bronze statue of Nero. The statue has been cast to look like a God. Linus wonders whether he really wants a guy with this cartoon ego as a partner? Linus enters the grounds after presenting his invitation to the guards. Nero's palace is called the Domus Aurea. It means the house of gold. But Linus notices that most of what is golden is really vast quantities of amber. It's imbedded in all parts of the building. It serves as a tasteful trim. The amber works better than gold. The light from the sun during the day and torches at night refract through the substance. Gold metal would not have been so alive. The amber originally came from the Black Sea area of the empire. There is also gold leaf. Nothing is too good for Nero. The palace grounds are sprawling. It covers approximately 150 acres. There was a convenient fire some years ago that freed up the land for Nero's country estate in metropolitan Rome. There are vineyards and fruit trees. Flocks of animals graze in fenced fields. Included on the property are magnificent landscaped areas spaced among reflection pools, sitting areas, pavilions and columned porticos. Nero's architects have had the Wonders of the World to learn from . . . Babylonians, Greeks, Egyptians, Persians, Corinthians etc. Distinct marble columns outline a man made lake. It also serve as a source of water for all the animal, fowl and birds. And all those peacocks are breathtaking. Guards are everywhere yet they are discreet. The whole complex is encircled by fifteen foot high and five foot thick walls.

As Linus approaches the main building, a servant

walks out to meet him. He speaks," Good morning my lord Linus. I am Petronius. I'm the emperors personal assistant. Please follow me. I will take you to the emperor."

Linus has heard of Petronius. He is the self acclaimed "Voluptuary in Residence and Adviser to Caesar On All Things Sensual." All these egos and caricatures worry Linus about the long term viability of Rome. Didn't Petronius publish a book describing one of Nero's parties? Yes he did. It was called *The Satyricon.* Parts of it were recited in the senate. It was part of a scathing critique of the excesses and costs of Emperor Nero's household.

Linus follows the servant to a side entrance. They enter a door and walk into a private garden. It's a small variation of the grounds that Linus just came through. Two fountains are separated by a pool of water with floating flowers. Birds are bathing. Some are being fed in another area. Linus looks closely. It's Nero. He's throwing feed around for the little birds. The servant asks Linus to wait. The servant goes to Nero and announces Linus and asks if there are any further instructions. Nero shakes his head no and dismisses the aid.

Nero approaches Linus. He is about the same height. He has light blond hair and a chubby face. His eyes are blue and a wee bit bloodshot. His upper torso slants away from his head. It reaches its fullest extent around the hips and then slants inward on top of skinny legs. Nero relies on skilled tailors to cover most of an unattractive body. He speaks, "Welcome Linus."

Linus responds with a bow and a greeting, "Hail Caesar. I am Linus from the Family Villanova. We come to serve you."

"Notice the birds Linus. They are hungry. I feed what I can. But some times birds from other parts of the city find out about the easy pickings here and they flock to this garden and muscle out my regulars. Some of the intruders are from far away counties. They are birds brought here by immigrants. Immigrants is a euphemism. I call immigrants riffraff. The rabble is engulfing Rome. They stream in daily. They stink. The pastures of my Domus Aurea are my only barrier from their air borne filth. I was born in Antium. I'm a simple country boy at heart. These grounds somewhat duplicate my childhood home. This is the only way I can bear to be Caesar. Sometimes I have to stop feeding all the birds. Only when my regulars persist and the foreign birds have moved elsewhere do I resume feeding. Rome is a crowed place. And everyone wants something to eat. If you take my meaning?"

"I do Caesar. Thank you again for seeing me. But I

do not come with my hand open for something. Rather I have a hand that is ready to offer. Your immigrant problem is like my deadbeat Christian problem. Together we can solve each others vexation."

"That's a novelty. Come sit with me Linus. Would you care for a drink? Something to eat perhaps?"

Caesar and Linus sit down in a pavilion that is covered in purple wisteria. The scent is breath taking. "No thank you Caesar. May I present my offer for your consideration?"

"Please do."

"We have a bone between us. It is call the Holy Roman Catholic Church. It's bone that can be used in two ways. We can club our enemies with it. But we can also chew on it for pleasure. Your senate allies in the pagan religion enterprise resent my church. We poach their believers. I understand that resentment. If I were they I would too. But they think of themselves first. No doubt they enlist your help in squeezing my church and its followers so that they may recoup some of the money that they have lost due to the attrition of pagan worshipers joining my Catholic Church. I don't know what they offer you. I really don't care. If you asked my advice, I would say 'Continue to accept the money from the pagan lobby.' My deal is separate. I offer a partnership. It will be with me and the Villanova Family. We offer Caesar half of our church enterprise."

"That is very generous. I assume the income and the prospects are worthwhile?"

"Truly Caesar. The income is as of today approximately 10,000 pieces a month. The prospects of the church in the greater Roman Empire are staggering if our test marketing indications prove true. "

Caesar is impressed, "How can you get so much from Rome?"

"With all do respect, Caesar. You have too much faith in what your pagan lobby allies say their take is. They may say that they take in only so much. And based on that figure your share is this. But in reality they take in 10 times that amount. And they pocket the difference. I propose an honest accounting. I propose and honest split on The Holy Roman Catholic Church income.."

"Go on."

"May I be so bold to offer Caesar a quick tutorial of the religion business?"

"Please proceed."

Linus relaxes and continues," The religion business is not like any other business. It touches people in places that other enterprises can't reach. It deals with an underground economy. Your tax collectors can't get to the underground economy. Donations and the selling of indulgences and other fee for religious service is not in the tax code. This is a new source of revenue that the Villanova Family is offering its emperor. It will be delivered to Caesar where he designates. It will be on a monthly basis. There will be expenses coupled with the expansion of the church. And as a partner Caesar would share those expenses. The money would be your own. Your imagination would be the only guide in spending a fortune. There would be no senators to butter up or shout down. Why would an emperor want to deal with mere politicians if he had another choice?"

"That sounds very interesting. But you must realize that our pagan religion has been around for thousands of years. It wouldn't be politically possible for me to embrace the Christian religion."

"Certainly Caesar. We understand your position. That's why we offer a silent partnership."

The emperor asks, "And what do you want from me?"

"We would appreciate the pressure on our recruiting and operations to be lifted. We can give you cover by giving you undesirables from within our organization for conscription into slavery or human sacrifices in gladiatorial games. We have Christians that only show up for food distributions. They don't do any work. You could make use of them in any way you see fit. One immediate triumph to show your pagan allies would be the capture and death of Peter. He is our Bishop of Rome. I am his heir. So any time is convenient for us. He has outlived his usefulness to the Villanova Family. Plus we do not want anymore Jews as Bishop of Rome. From now on it will only be Italians or their designated representatives. We also offer Caesar a service of eliminating pagan allies or any other allies he feels need to be removed. No one will suspect you. No one will suspect us. It will be a miracle." Linus smiles.

The emperor asks, "You mentioned that you and the Villanova Family could help me with my immigrant problem. How could that be done?"

"Many of your undesirable immigrants are in fact our new Christian converts. As I said earlier, we are appalled by some of them as you are. We can arrange for their arrests by your Centurians. We can also monitor truly subversive Christian immigrants and help you mitigate the crime waves that have infested Rome."

Nero asks, "What of this political revolution and sedition that is the implied message of the Holy Roman Catholic Church? It's the same as the dreaded democracy. Only it's worse because of the religious right of equality it preaches. How can we let a little poison trickle into our body politic and not be concerned? The poison builds up and eventually we die."

"That's true Caesar. The Catholic Church at it's core is subversive. It would sweep away all the stands in its way. It would sweep Caesar and Rome away. Look at it this way. We have two choices. We can manage the expectations of the coming deluge of scum from the provinces which some part will be Christian ? Or does Caesar want to try to kill all the new arrivals by himself? Some of those new arrivals will be exploitable and valued Christians. They will be a new undercover army in waiting. They will also be valued donation-giving and work-pledging customers of Caesar's new business arrangement. They can also be persuaded to take up arms against non-Christians that also happen to be enemies of Caesar. In short my Caesar, What's wrong with playing both sides? Those are the games I like to play. We can't lose."

Nero comments, "You have certainly thought about everything. My compliments to you and the Villanova Family. Let me think on it. I think we should never see each other again in the palace. This place has spies everywhere. Some of their spies can read lips at 20 feet. They don't have to be in ear shot. It's not the private secure place one might think. We need a liaison. Petronius will contact this liaison."

Linus answers, "I have just the right man for the job. His name is Niccolo Machiavelli. He will go far. I never met a man with so many self serving views of a situation. And it can be so civilized but lethal and profitable. I will tell him to work out a communication routine with Petronius."

In a few years Peter would be dead. He would be crucified upside down. A year after Peter died, Nero would take his own life to thwart numerous assassination attempts. Nero was the last of the Julian-Claudian dynasty. That was a total of six Caesars. Of that six only three died of natural causes. They were Augustus, Tiberius and Claudius. Two others were assassinated They were Julius Caesar and Caligula. Nero committed suicide under threat of assassination. There were a total of 95 Caesars of the Roman Empire which started with Julius in the 1st Century B.C. and ended with Justin II in 6th century A.D. Of that total only 32 died of a natural cause. The other 63 were either assassinated or died in combat fighting political rivals. The assassins were mostly the Praetorian guard in cahoots with the Senate. It would be hard to make a convincing argument for one to aspire to be Emperor given those scores. While we are at it. Anyone who wants to be God or is mistaken for one has even less odds in his favor. Light comedy always offers refuge for the world weary. The light heart triumphs over the famous, the religious and the wealthy. Without any particular talent the light of heart endure and enjoy.

Epilogue

In this book's first chapter the imperious, world weary Roman Governor Pontius Pilate addresses Jesus, "The only thing more over rated than man is his over rated Gods. Now I am informed that you are both man and God. I am rhetorically speechless." Pilate pauses theatrically. Then like an eagle in a stoop towards a hapless rabbit he glares at Jesus and says, "Please guide me through your marvelous hybrid being."

The book starts with the judgment and death of Jesus Christ. His death on the cross is one of the most known facts in recorded history. It's been recorded in books. It's been depicted in paintings. It's been sculpted. It has been an oral tradition. Ergo why bother to build to a climax when we all know how it ends. And yet the characters in this book that participate in the trial of Jesus are fully human with the good and the bad and the true traits in full cartoon. The main story is about what brought Jesus to this unhappy end. Because the life of Jesus before his death is something that is fertile ground for dramatization and speculation, one might say that the Bible covers his life also. But since the Bible took hundreds of years to organize and edit, one suspects there were no opportunities overlooked to gloss over some facts that pointed to Jesus being a mere human. The editors of the Bible had an incentive to reinforce a divine Jesus. He and they needed that kind of heavenly credibility to be a worthy founder of their Catholic Church. Christ was nothing if not controversial. And man is nothing if not two sided.

The religious teachings of Christ that formed the Catholic Church are found recorded in the Bible. But the Bible is made up of the NEW TESTAMENT and the OLD TESTAMENT. That split personality fact of the Bible is enough to cause questions, because some of the OLD TESTAMENT loyalists are the ones who argued for the death of Jesus. Indeed the Bible has something for every one. The OLD TESTAMENT part of the Bible claims the Jews are the "chosen people." The NEW TESTAMENT claims "all are children of God." The OLD TESTAMENT instructs "an eye for an eye" in retaliation.

The NEW TESTAMENT advises "turn the other cheek." OLD TESTAMENT followers brought Jesus before Pilate for the death penalty. NEW TESTAMENT followers not only wanted Jesus spared but claimed he was the son of God. And to top it all off is the gospel of Saint John. That gospel includes the Book of Revelations also known as the Apocalypse. John writes that in his dream he is told a "New Jerusalem" is coming along with the promised Messiah who is the son of God. Among other hair raising events actually dreamed by the apostle John will be the slaughter of all non-Christian Jews by an angel of God! And yet America professes to have a "Judeo-Christian Ethic." Then it's no wonder that we have so many lawyers and litigation. No matter what the contentious issue, everyone can find Gods support some where in the Bible. As a book, the Bible lacked an editor for credibility. As a source of controversy and popularity it obviously has something going for it. I'm writing about it today in an effort to show how things got off track between Jesus and his church and to flesh out the human Jesus.

Probably the biggest pluses for the Bible are the dates of its publication and the market it served. The OLD TESTAMENT was ancient. It's piece meal publication started in the 1300 B.C. But the beginnings of the NEW

TESTAMENT started in 35 A.D. with the writings of the apostles. Those apostolic writings comprise the critical must-be-believed canon of the Catholic Church. The apostles lived with Jesus in real time. But later on after most were dead there were also councils that convened to determine what the apostles meant in their writings. And that includes revisiting what Jesus meant when he spoke. It was done by people who were not present. So the canon of the Bible has been edited by non witness. And that's OK? And here is where things can get lost in translation. Or things can be put into translations. Its an area for mischief. To be fair it can be honest mischief or dishonest mischief.

Examples of that later tweaking of the Bibles original content and meaning include but are not limited to the Council of Jerusalem in 50 A.D.. That was sixteen years after the death of Christ. The Council instructed the newcomers, both Jews and Gentiles, to Christ's religion about the do and don't along with a quick tutorial on Jesus' background. The Council of Jerusalem advocated the laws of Abraham and Moses: don't steal; don't kill; don't covet a neighbors wife; etc. But it also addressed the question of circumcision. Should gentiles be forced to undergo the procedure or should it be non compulsory? It was decided that it would be encouraged but not made compulsory. Rabbis were hired to perform a circumcision. So it was a fee for service event. Monetizing religious services was only one key difference between Jesus and the church that claimed to follow his teachings. Jesus advocated private worship. He wasn't about large cathedrals or conspicuous worship. Whether he was divine or not his original religion was private. But there were too many special interests in the Old Testament to let the New Testament blot them all out. So the editors of the Bible presented them as one. Again, Jesus' message was simple. The people who ran his church after he was gone changed the personal religion to a catholic or universal religion. Can a simple religion really scale up to the universal level and still stay simple and personal? There's no money or power in personal faith. That type of private quiet worship can be done without cathedrals or scurrying priests. The church, on the other hand, is complete with an extensive bureaucracy of power, collection points for money of all denominations and the mummery of all kinds of church services and fees for service.

Barter was also encouraged. Small and large tracts of land for a perpetual indulgence would also get you to the front pews of worshipers. Such large gifts might also get you a position in the church hierarchy so others might be encouraged to copy. Other Catholic Church councils included the Council of Nicaea convened in 325 A.D. by the Emperor Constantine. It resolved what the apostles meant by the phrase "Jesus is one with God his father." According to the Council that phrase meant he was the same in divinity. Another was the Council of Trent convened in December, 13, 1545. It was in and out of session until December 4, 1563. That's over 18 years being used to untangle or tangle what Christ's teachings were and what the Catholic Church said they were. That is not necessarily the same thing. One important ruling that came from the Trent Council was the proclamation that Catholic Church had exclusive rights to interpret the Bible. That shut down all dialogue. If any one else tried to reinterpret the Bible he or she would be branded as a heretic.

An example of how seriously the church protected its franchise and what it meant in the extreme to be labeled a heretic can be seen in the case of Giordano Bruno. In 1600 the fifty-two year old Bruno was burned at the stake for heresy. He was a mathematician, philosopher and astronomer who also believed in Jesus being the son of God. He was also a friar in the

Dominican Order. What was his heresy? He theorized that the sun was a star and that the universe contained an infinite number of other intelligent beings. He was brought before a Roman Inquisition and found guilty of teaching things not found in the Bible and also accused of promoting pantheism. The Inquisition panel was correct about not finding myriad other intelligent beings being posited in the Bible. But by the same logic, how did the Inquisition panel get the authority to judge heresy about something that wasn't in the Bible? Such is the evil natural progression of events aided by absolute heavenly and secular power. If the Catholic Church could demonize Giordano Bruno than almost anybody could be fair game. Church history is filled with witch hunts, both actual and figuratively. The Inquisition also "refined" church teachings on the sacraments, salvation and biblical canon.

It branded Martin Luther as a heretic, but at the same time condemned the Catholic Church's simony policy which was Luther's main objection. So Luther was vindicated but was branded a heretic for his methods. Any "religious" organization that is still redefining itself more than 1500 years after the simple but martyred founder is gone prompts thoughts that the church may have some time long ago lost its way.

To add insult to well meaning followers of Jesus, the church threatens excommunication to anyone who dares quibble over translations and interpretations. It would appear that organizational pie charts and chains of command now have at least half of the clerical focus and value. Any religion that is simple is harder to monetize. A simple religion wont make anyone rich in worldly assets. Fee for service is the way to go.

The church's mass market was the Roman Empires occupied territories. That was the de facto known world. The take away message of the writers of the NEW TESTAMENT was the implied fact that from birth all Gods children are equal. That had far reaching implications. It turned conventional views upside down. This also implied that every one should have the vote and be represented in a new different kind of representative government that was more liberal. It resembled the Greek democratic model but with a heavenly origin. The founders of the Catholic Church coupled religious rule with secular rule. This was unlike Jesus who famously said, "Render to Caesar what belongs to Caesar." Jesus was for separation of church and state.

The Greek democracy was an anathema to the founders of Rome's republic in 773 B.C. They wanted no part of it for the obvious reason that the "have nots" always outnumber the "haves" and it's only a matter of time before no one wants to work or save. It's easier to vote for your daily bread than bake it. The new Catholic philosophy instructed that we had to help people who were worse off than us. Charity wasn't a new idea. But mandated charity was. Using the tax system to redistribute wealth was new. It used as an example the differences between the occupiers and the occupied as a matter of guilt and shame. It was an irresistible implied call to arms against the Roman occupiers. The call to arms was both violent and nonviolent. The peoples of the earth now had a God who was on their side — a God greater than any earth bound Caesar. People who were previously known by their differences were now claiming to be equal. If one was poor, then one had prima facie evidence of an injustice. And there would be hell to pay if it wasn't put right. The pugnacious liberalism of the church was one of the reasons the Roman Empire fell. With every one in the empire in line for a vote it was only a matter of time before there was nothing left to share. And why pay taxes if the money and product went to a foreign country?

Whether the passages of the Bible are accurate or not, they serve the purpose of presenting Christ and his church as one and the same. Still, over 2000 years of recorded history have shown that at an early stage the actions of the Catholic Church deviated from the teachings of Christ. Examples include but are definitely not limited to the Inquisition, the Holy Wars and the selling of indulgences. All these atrocities were done in Christ's name. The popes of the Catholic Church spoke ex cathedra on matters of faith and morals. They spoke on behalf of Jesus. The quoted words of Christ in the gospels make no mention of approving wars, torture or selling religious favors. Indeed there is one church. And there was only one Christ. They are known by their differences.

Christ's divinity is a matter for debate. Gottfried Leibniz the 18th century German philosopher and mathematician wrote that Jesus was suspected of being the illegitimate son of a Roman officer from Calabria, Italy and of the biblical Mary. Christ's teachings were somewhat new to western civilization. They taught that we all have obligations from God to do unto others what we would have them do unto us. That succinct Golden Rule really says it all about Christ's teachings. Today the Catholic Church is anything but simple. The Church blurred or shaded Jesus' Golden Rule proverb and made it somewhat compulsory. The church's history is filled with schemes to monetize church power and grow in political power using Christ's as a front. These money making schemes have included simony which helped spark the 16th century Protestant Reformation.

This book treats Jesus and his Catholic Church in a cheeky, satiric manner. No apologies are necessary to Jesus if he is who they say he is, because all truly good people have a sense of humor. But Jesus was a man and therefore he had to have human characteristics and traits so as to be taken seriously by the people he engaged. He had to be recognized as human. Selling ideas or having a meaningful relationship with a group of followers requires a credible presentation in all aspects. Even messengers who are from God have to be appealing and understood. Jesus had to have a way of speaking in delivering his message. It had to be persuasive or he would have flopped. Those are by definition a sine qua non. So the characters in this book are presented in a human way. The person that the Bible presents as Jesus is stiff and a bore. He is too preachy. He's too philosophical. Those characteristics would turn off the common folks. They don't want to know about philosophy. It wouldn't help real people get through their day. Many wouldn't even know what Jesus was talking about. The Bible doesn't describe a physical Jesus. How tall was he? Was he stocky or slim? How did Jesus dress? What did he eat? Did he drink? What did he think of women? What did women think of him? Was he handsome? How did he do his hair? What did the men think of Jesus? Did they ask themselves, "What's this guy up to?" Did Jesus ever laugh? What kind of person never laughs? The lack of complete human details is suspicious. It really speaks about a too didactic, religious approach. Or is it a devious approach because of what's left out? Or does it indicate sloppiness which implies a credibility gap on accuracy in reporting? This raises the next question. How accurate were Jesus' "miracles" reported? Jesus was presented with only one face. He was presented by the founders of the church as a one-eyed jack. Only the stern glower of Jesus with his "you better do this or there will be hell to pay message" without comic relief was pushed by the church. That's a bore.

So Christ must have had some animal magnetism. He was a mammal. So what was he like? Hollywood introduced a good looking, but stiff and boring Jesus. The Hollywood casting directors knew how to attractively populate a screen, but their screenwriters must have been descended from the original apostles. They carried on the bland, didactic Christ. Maybe they were timid of treating Christ in a too familiar manner? Many of the screenwriters were Jewish or under Jewish supervision. Hollywood films was largely a Jewish funded business. The Jews did not want to be accused of any perceived disrespect to Jesus, as their relatives may have been part of the downtown Sanhedrin in biblical times. That was the hierarchy of the Jewish religion that demanded that open air, country Christ be crucified. It's still about selling tickets! The moguls of Hollywood didn't want controversy they wanted full seats. Only the good looks of motion picture stars and the secondary stories of love, hate and drama made biblical epics entertaining.

Christ's message was pretty basic. It just reiterated the common sense conclusion: treat others as you would be treated. But he did have some off message days. In Matthew, Chapter 10, Verse 34-39, he is reported saying, *"Do not think that I have come to send peace upon the earth. I have come to bring a sword not peace. For I have come to set a man at variance with his father and a daughter with her mother and a daughter in law with her mother in law. And a mans enemies will be of his own household. He who loves father or mother more than me is not worthy of me and he who loves son or daughter more than me is not worthy of me. And he who does not take up his cross and follow me is not worthy of me. He who finds his life will lose it and he who loses his life will find it."*

There were different sermon topics, but most boiled down to the Golden Rule. There may be a an argument for Christ's divinity because of his teachings. But at the same time those pushing his divinity had a compelling self interest to set up Jesus as divine so that they could set up and run a church that would carry on the saving of souls after he left. That takes organization and requires a hierarchy of management, physical structures, props and a cash flow. The church is a lucrative and powerful body complete with its own tailored guidelines of political and holy correctness that carry eternal damnation as the forfeit. Religious political correctness can demonize whole races of people, foment wars and confiscate lands. Missionary work spread Christ's teaching to new lands. They were a cost effective way of putting new areas on the map and into the hands of the greedy European royalty and corsairs that operated on commission. Kings and Queens and peers would happily kick in naval and military support so as to partner with the church's land office business.

Down through the ages Popes were almost always from politically connected and wealthy royal families, including the Borgia, who were after more wealth and power. That arguably made the pope the go-to-guy for the most powerful one-stop-seat-of-power on the planet. He commanded the secular and the spiritual. Pope Alexander VI (1492-1503) was the first papal head who was openly recognized to have had children with his lovers. He fathered four and possibly eleven children. His notorious brood included Caesar, Giovanni, Lucrezia and Gioffre Borgia. Pope Alexander VI was connected by the marriage of a relation to the Duke of Milan Ludovico Sforza's family, the same Duke that commissioned Leonardo da Vinci to paint the Last Supper. That famous painting was also controversial because of the inclusion of a very feminine Mary Magdalene seated next to Jesus. Alexander VI dealt with the Sforza Family routinely. Together with the Medici Family they were the plutocratic cartel that ran anything of economic importance in Italy. One wonders if Alexander VI tried to do a little positive PR to offset his poor public image by having Sforza arrange with da Vinci the juxtaposition of Mary with Jesus and indicate the Savior also had a taste for the ladies.

Recently there's some new bad news for the Catholic Church. The scandals regarding sexual predation rife through the priestly ranks suggests the Catholic

243

Church brushes up against RICO (Racketeer Influenced Corrupt Organizations Act) statutes as a result of its part in the constructively criminal systemic sexual predation of youth and the cover ups by higher ups that followed. This may be a stretch, but lesser crimes by lesser organizations have been treated more harshly. These sensational sexual predation revelations are a fact and blot that go back decades. In short, the church resembles more a modern day multinational business than a humble saver of souls. And it plays fast and loose with law and common sense custom.

The 19th century philosopher and classical language philologist Friedrich Nietzsche said, "The first, last and only Christian was Jesus Christ." The others that followed him in the hierarchy of the church he called lurking "hall spiders."